The car lurched forward

A Honda scooter spurted ahead, almost raising its front wheel off the ground. The passenger no longer had his arms around the driver's waist. He leaned to the left as the Honda raced toward the car.

"Down!" Bolan shouted, shoving the driver away from the wheel.

"What the hell are you doing?" Bishop roared.

The Executioner drew the Beretta and turned to the side window. The Honda was ten feet away now, the passenger grinning. He leveled an Uzi, and his intention was clear.

Bolan fired through the glass, but the scooter was too quick. The enemy gunner let loose a sustained burst that shattered both windows on the passenger side of the Buick.

The warrior shoved his door open and tumbled into the street, rolled and came up firing. His first shot slammed into the driver. The second punctured the small gas tank.

People had begun to scream, and they tried to run, but the narrow street was jammed. The bike went over, its exhaust scraping the asphalt. Sparks ignited the geyser of fuel.

In slow motion, the flame chewed its way back toward the tank....

D1005555

MACK BOLAN®

The Executioner

#115 Circle of Steel
#116 The Killing Urge
#117 Vendetta in Venice
#118 Warrior's Revenge
#119 Line of Fire
#120 Border Sweep
#121 Twisted Path
#122 Desert Strike
#123 War Born
#124 Night Kill
#125 Dead Man's Tale
#126 Death Wind
#127 Kill Zone
#128 Sudan Slaughter
#129 Haitian Hit
#130 Dead Line
#131 Ice Wolf
#132 The Big Kill
#133 Blood Run
#134 White Line War
#135 Devil Force
#136 Down and Dirty
#137 Battle Lines
#138 Kill Trap
#139 Cutting Edge
#140 Wild Card
#141 Direct Hit
#142 Fatal Error
#143 Helldust Cruise
#144 Whipsaw
#145 Chicago Payoff
#146 Deadly Tactics
#147 Payback Game
#148 Deep and Swift
#149 Blood Rules
#150 Death Load

Stony Man Doctrine
Terminal Velocity
Resurrection Day
Dirty War
Flight 741
Dead Easy
Sudden Death
Rogue Force
Tropic Heat
Fire in the Sky
Anvil of Hell
Flash Point
Flesh and Blood
Moving Target
Tightrope
Blowout
Blood Fever
Knockdown
Assault
Backlash
Siege
Blockade
Evil Kingdom

DON PENDLETON'S

THE EXECUTIONER®

FEATURING MACK BOLAN®

DEATH LOAD

First edition June 1991

ISBN 0-373-61150-1

Special thanks and acknowledgment to
Charlie McDade for his contribution to this work.

DEATH LOAD

Copyright © 1991 by Worldwide Library.
Philippine copyright 1991. Australian copyright 1991.

All rights reserved. Except for use in any review, the
reproduction or utilization of this work in whole or in part
in any form by any electronic, mechanical or other means,
now known or hereafter invented, including xerography,
photocopying and recording, or in any information storage
or retrieval system, is forbidden without the permission
of the publisher, Worldwide Library, 225 Duncan Mill Road,
Don Mills, Ontario, Canada M3B 3K9.

All the characters in this book have no existence outside the
imagination of the author and have no relation whatsoever to
anyone bearing the same name or names. They are not even
distantly inspired by any individual known or unknown to the
author, and all the incidents are pure invention.

® and TM are trademarks of the publisher. MACK BOLAN,
GOLD EAGLE, WORLDWIDE LIBRARY and the GLOBE DESIGN
are registered in the United States Patent and Trademark Office and
in other countries.

Printed in U.S.A.

Injustice anywhere is a threat to justice everywhere.

—Martin Luther King, Jr.
1929–1968

There is no such thing as justice—in or out of court.

—Clarence Seward Darrow
1857–1938

They say that all men are equal before the law. Well, some men think they're above the law. And that is arrogance of the highest order. When the acts of such men cost innocent lives, the perpetrators must pay the supreme price.

—Mack Bolan

THE MACK BOLAN® LEGEND

Nothing less than a war could have fashioned the destiny of the man called Mack Bolan. Bolan earned the Executioner title in the jungle hell of Vietnam.

But this soldier also wore another name—Sergeant Mercy. He was so tagged because of the compassion he showed to wounded comrades-in-arms and Vietnamese civilians.

Mack Bolan's second tour of duty ended prematurely when he was given emergency leave to return home and bury his family, victims of the Mob. Then he declared a one-man war against the Mafia.

He confronted the Families head-on from coast to coast, and soon a hope of victory began to appear. But Bolan had broken society's every rule. That same society started gunning for this elusive warrior—to no avail.

So Bolan was offered amnesty to work within the system against terrorism. This time, as an employee of Uncle Sam, Bolan became Colonel John Phoenix. With a command center at Stony Man Farm in Virginia, he and his new allies—Able Team and Phoenix Force—waged relentless war on a new adversary: the KGB.

But when his one true love, April Rose, died at the hands of the Soviet terror machine, Bolan severed all ties with Establishment authority.

Now, after a lengthy lone-wolf struggle and much soul-searching, the Executioner has agreed to enter an "arm's-length" alliance with his government once more, reserving the right to pursue personal missions in his Everlasting War.

PROLOGUE

Lieutenant Bodorn Salang stared at the slight woman before him, at a loss to understand why representatives of Western do-gooder organizations insisted on visiting the refugee camps. But he'd been told to cooperate, so he would.

"Very well, if you insist on going to the camp at Chulingorn, I have no choice. Are you sure you want to do this?"

She nodded.

"It can be dangerous, you know."

"I appreciate that. But my concern is for the refugees. If there's anything that can be done for them, I want to make sure it gets done. To do that, I have to see for myself what I'll be talking about."

Three jeeps were already waiting, their engines running. Two were occupied by Thai soldiers, while the middle jeep, obviously intended for her and Salang, had a vacant rear seat. The driver and the soldier next to him were no less heavily armed than the other eight men.

Katherine wondered whether the protection was necessary. "Do we need all these soldiers? I thought Chulingorn was secure."

"The camps are extremely dangerous places. We have to worry about external forces who attack our soldiers. As long as you are my responsibility, I'll see to it that you're safe. The Khmer Rouge occasionally come into Thai territory and . . . I suppose you could call it kidnap—they call it 'liberate'—groups of refugees."

"You can't be serious." She couldn't let him know just how much she knew. It was hard pretending to be so helpless, so naive. But it was necessary.

"I absolutely am."

"But why?"

Salang shrugged, turned away and climbed into the jeep. Settling himself in the seat, he waited for her to climb in before answering. "Slave labor, I guess."

"And you let them do it?"

"Thailand is a big country. The border is long, and the army is small. And what goes on in the jungle in this part of the world is of little interest to anyone."

"It's of interest to me, Lieutenant, and to my organization. Shall we go?"

Salang barked an order, and the lead jeep stuttered into motion. All three vehicles crawled through the gate of the military post and were swallowed almost immediately by the jungle.

Bugs swarmed out of the vegetation, gathering around their heads. Some smacked against the windshields, their brittle hulls popping and cracking. It was everything Katherine May remembered and more. It had been two years since she'd last been in Thailand, and what Salang didn't know—because she didn't want him to know—was that she had herself been a resident of the Khao-i-Dang refugee camp for four months in 1978. They had been the four longest months of her twenty-nine years.

Salang was typical, so she didn't take it personally. It was understandable, to a degree, that the Thai people would resent the flood of bruised humanity suddenly swept across the border. But humanity demanded they do something about the horror. World opinion, however, was less than excited about the situation, and without it there was little likelihood that Thais, or anyone else for that matter, would do any more than the minimal they were already doing. That there was a centuries-old history of hatred between the two peoples did nothing to spur the Bangkok government to humanitarian effort.

Katherine May felt like a fraud. In a way, she was a fraud, but it was for a higher purpose, and that should have made it easier. But it didn't. Under the cover of a field representative of the World Refugee Council, she'd come back to the edge of hell many times, not to examine the conditions in the camps, but to gather information for her real employer, the Intelligence Division of the U.S. State Department.

But she'd left all that behind. She couldn't avoid seeing the horror and thinking that somehow all the cloak-and-dagger business in the world would never make things better. So she had quit. Really and truly. She'd thrown herself into her cover work with missionary zeal.

Until Bishop called.

"Just one more," he'd said. Not even pleading, he'd assumed she'd do it, and made the arrangements even before speaking to her. And he'd been right. But this, she promised herself, was the last time.

She was supposed to make contact with an agent who had slipped into the camp from the interior of Cambodia and who, once he'd passed the information gathered over a six-month period, would slip back over the border. She gave an involuntary shudder just thinking about it.

The trees thinned on the right now, and Katherine saw water through the undergrowth, bright patches of sun on the greenish-brown surface.

Salang pointed and said, "The Mun. Or rather a branch of it. Not far now."

A thin haze of gray smoke wafted through the trees, its sharp tang reaching Katherine's nostrils a few seconds later. Fires at the camp, no doubt. And then came the thick, too-sweet smell of food laced with spices, tasteless pap disguised as nourishment, dosed heavily with anything strong enough to make it palatable. She remembered it only too well, the lumpy cassava mush so full of curry it seemed to peel the skin off the mouth and tongue as it was swallowed. She almost gagged.

They broke through the trees, and suddenly there it was—a jumble of tents and makeshift shelters, everything from thatched huts to shacks made of packing crates and rusted tin. It looked like she remembered, only worse.

The stench washed over her in a thick wave. The human waste, the rotting food, the smell of thousands of unwashed bodies crammed into a few acres was overwhelming. The people milled around, talking among themselves, or to themselves, babies squalled and older children darted through the wasteland like rats, shouting unintelligibly.

The jeeps stopped at the barbed wire gate, then nudged on through like cattle entering a slaughterhouse pen. They stopped in front of the one permanent building in the center of the camp, which served as army headquarters and administrative post for the meager assistance trickling through the world's charitable organizations and filtered through the Thai government.

Katherine May climbed out of the jeep into the mud. She walked toward the board porch of the building, her feet being sucked into the muck. It felt as if something were trying to swallow her boots, rip them from her feet to get at her flesh. It made her skin crawl. Bugs skittered over the swirling yellowish water and tried to climb up her legs. She stamped her feet as best she could and climbed onto the porch.

A buzz suddenly erupted on one edge of the camp, and everyone turned toward the commotion.

The sudden explosion of gunfire drew the troops out of the main building. Katherine was knocked to the ground, landing on her back in the mud. Salang glanced at her, then sprinted toward the sound of the shooting.

Katherine struggled to her feet and sprinted after him. "What's happening?" she asked.

"Probably Khmer Rouge."

"What?"

"You heard me. I already told you that they raid every once in a while and force a couple of hundred people to follow them back across the border."

"But why? Why now, today?"

The lieutenant didn't really understand the question, not the way she meant it. "If I knew that..." Salang shrugged. The gunfire had subsided for a few moments, and Katherine was beginning to think it was a false alarm. She had to find Trang, her contact, but where?

Salang ran toward the back perimeter of the camp, and she followed him. More gunshots, less furious this time, cracked and echoed off the surrounding forest. The swirls of terrified people rushing past were just a blur. Trang wouldn't run, she thought. Or would he?

Salang muscled his way through a knot of soldiers, standing with their rifles aimed toward a small band of guerrillas. Katherine pushed past him and shouted at the guerrillas. Behind them, a small group of men and women was visible among the trees. The fence had been cut, and the tight coils of razor wire had curled into dense spirals against the nearest post on either side of the cut.

Salang called to her, but she ignored him, charging toward the guerrillas and shouting in what the lieutenant recognized as Khmer.

One of the guerrillas stepped away from the others, sauntering forward, his face a mask of stone. Katherine continued to run, finally stopping and planting herself no more then five feet away from him. He stood there, an AK-47 crooked over one arm, his finger curled lazily through the trigger guard.

"Where are you taking those people?" she demanded.

"I'm not taking them anywhere. They're going home to Cambodia."

"You can't do that. You can't force people against their will."

"I'm not forcing anyone. They're Cambodian. They're going home where they belong. By the way, where did you learn to speak Khmer?" he asked abruptly.

"I'm Cambodian," she replied, and his manner changed almost immediately. "You have no right to do this." Even as Katherine said it, she realized just how feeble an objection it was. Behind him, several of the guerrillas had moved a few feet closer. Beyond them, Katherine could see the backs of the last few refugees disappearing into the undergrowth.

She felt a hand on her shoulder and realized Salang had finally joined her. He tugged at her sleeve, trying to get her to return to safety with him. When she jerked free, the guerrilla fired a short burst into the dirt. The slugs narrowly missed Salang's legs, and the guerrilla grinned.

In awkward Thai he said, "Explain to the woman how it is."

Katherine turned to Salang, who shrugged helplessly. "He's right," he said. "There is nothing we can do."

Salang started to back up, begging Katherine to come with him. Instead, she leaped forward and slapped the guerrilla sharply across the face. He barked a command, and several of his men stepped forward to grab the woman, dragging her away.

She screamed, and Salang took a step forward, but a wall of rifles suddenly blocked his path. He tried to force his way through, and a rifle butt caught him high on the side of the head. He fell to one knee.

"You can't take her," Salang said. "She's with the World Refugee Council."

The leader smiled again. "Let them come get her. In the meantime, perhaps she'll learn some manners."

Salang watched helplessly as the guerrillas, their rifles ready, backed toward the trees. One by one they melted into the forest. A minute later they were gone.

The lieutenant knew he was in big trouble.

Chogram Thant stared at the three men sitting across from him. He wasn't happy, and he made no attempt to disguise that fact.

Finally he cleared his throat. "Miss May has put my government in a difficult position, and you didn't help, Lieutenant." His eyes bored into Salang.

"It wasn't entirely her fault," the lieutenant replied. "She—"

"The assessment of blame isn't the province of a soldier. That is a diplomatic concern, and none of yours."

He turned to the two other men in the room, both American. "Mr. Bishop, I hope your man here is better at discharging his responsibilities."

Clayton Bishop nodded.

"I hope so. Now, I want the entire story on Miss May. I don't think, inside this room, we need concern ourselves any further with the rather flimsy mythology used to justify her presence in Thailand."

Bishop knit his brows. "I don't understand."

"Of course you do. You understand quite well. Before we go any further I want the truth—not a fall-back version, either. I want the plain, unvarnished truth. And I think it only fair to warn you that I'm not easily deceived."

Bishop sighed. He'd been prepared for this eventuality and had the authority, by delegation, to tell the truth, but he was trying to decide whether he had to. He ran the considerable risk, if he tried his alternate cover, that Thant not only wouldn't accept it, but that he wouldn't subsequently accept the actual truth, either. That would make what was already a mess, messier still.

He looked at the man next to him, thought a moment longer, then asked, "Can we talk alone?"

Thant smiled. "Of course."

Salang stood and moved toward the door. The second American stayed where he was, and Thant glared at him. "Mr. Bishop and I wish to discuss this matter in private," he said, leaning back and waiting for the big American to follow Salang out of the room.

He was doomed to be disappointed. "I'm staying. I've had enough of diplomatic courtesy. I have a job to do, and I want the whole story."

Thant stood abruptly. "Then I'm afraid this meeting is at an end."

"Fine by me."

Bishop raised a hand. "Not so fast. Mr. Thant, can I have a word with you?"

Thant nodded. "Very well."

Bishop stood and tugged the Thai official into one corner of his huge office. Mack Bolan sat and watched them playing at conspiracy like schoolboys. Thant was listening closely, leaning toward the taller Bishop and nodding. Bishop glanced at his countryman once, turned back to Thant and extended his hand.

Bishop walked back to his seat. "You can stay."

"Shall we begin?" Thant asked.

"Not yet," Bolan said. "I want Lieutenant Salang here, too."

Bishop sighed in exasperation. "You can't tell—"

"Get him."

Thant was on the verge of exploding.

Bolan stood. "Look, you're going to ask me to go into the Cambodian jungle to find Katherine May, right?"

Bishop nodded.

The Executioner turned to Thant. "And you're going to send Lieutenant Salang with me?"

Thant started to protest, then seemed to think better of it. He wasn't used to such plain speaking, but the man had a point. "Yes, I'm going to send Lieutenant Salang with you."

The American nodded. "I can't speak for him, but I'll tell you that I'm not going anywhere without knowing the 'unvarnished' truth, as you put it. And I won't ask anyone else to go without that knowledge. You can't send a man out blind and ask him to do your dirty work."

"But if you know, why does he have to know?" Thant argued.

"Because I could get killed out there. So could he. We have the right to know why."

Thant looked at Bishop hopelessly. "Does he have the right to refuse?"

The big American answered for himself. "You bet I do."

Bishop nodded in agreement. "Yes, he does."

Thant caved in. "Lieutenant?"

Salang stuck his head through the doorway. "Sir?"

"Come in, and close the door behind you, please." Thant sank into a chair behind his desk.

Salang resumed his seat, looking confused and a little irritated.

"Very well, then, Mr. Bishop," Thant said. "Please begin."

Bishop took a deep breath. "A little background. As you know, China is still giving aid and comfort to the Khmer Rouge. There are all sorts of rumors, but hard information is difficult to come by. As near as we can tell, Pol Pot is still in charge, although there are indications that the Khmer Rouge may have begun to fragment. China ignores world opinion for the most part, but Pol Pot might be too much of a liability even for the Chinese. The Vietnamese have officially withdrawn, but I emphasize officially. They're nervous about Pol Pot, and about China. Until there's some sort of negotiated settlement, and even after, there will be jockeying for position. Neither China nor Vietnam wants Cambodia, Kampuchea, or whatever the new rulers decide to call it, in the other's corner."

Thant rapped his knuckles on the desk. "This is old news, Mr. Bishop, and I don't see what it has to do with the current problem."

"I'm getting to that."

"Please hurry. Otherwise my successor will have to hear the conclusion."

"All right, I'll try to condense."

"Please do. And please include something of relevance to Miss Katherine May and this unfortunate situation she has precipitated."

"Ms. May was more than a field-worker for the World Refugee Council."

"Again, old news," Thant said. "That was obvious. Please, though, tell us what *else* she was."

"She was working with Vietnamese intelligence on our behalf. And, through back channels, for the Intelligence Division of the U.S. State Department."

"I assume, then, she wasn't on vacation when she went to visit the refugee camp at Chulingorn."

Bishop glared at Thant, who beamed beatifically. But he continued. "The Vietnamese have a string of agents inside the Khmer Rouge. They are, for the most part, Cambodians who were raised in Vietnam. Ms. May was supposed to make contact with one of these agents at the camp. The agent in question periodically slipped across the border to make such contact, then would reinfiltrate the KR. As to what happened at the camp, I can't guess. I don't know why Katherine would have done what she did. Maybe Lieutenant Salang can help." Bishop turned to the soldier. "If I understand correctly, you'd just arrived when the trouble started."

Salang nodded. "That's correct. Miss May hadn't even checked into the office when the Khmer Rouge attacked. They do it all the time, raiding by driving two or three hundred people back across the border."

"Could the agent she was to meet have been one of those taken?"

"I suppose so. But I don't know how she could have known that. There wasn't time. It wasn't possible to see the faces of any of those taken. They were at the far edge of the camp, and we never got close enough. At least I don't think so."

"You've got to be sure, Lieutenant. Thinking so isn't good enough. You must be certain."

"I'm certain, Mr. Bishop. She couldn't have."

"Could she have been told by someone else that her contact had been taken?"

"No. She never spoke to anyone. There wasn't time. It all happened so quickly."

"Describe for me exactly what happened."

Salang sighed. "We'd just reached the headquarters building when gunfire broke out. I knew right away what it was, and I think she did, too. I ran toward the point of attack, and she was right behind me. A number of the guerrillas were watching the rear while the rest herded the refugees into the jungle. Miss May got into an argument with the apparent leader, then he dragged her into the jungle. I don't know why. They were arguing in Khmer, so I don't know what they were saying. We went after them and ran into an ambush."

"Like they expected you to follow them?" Bolan asked.

He thought for a moment before answering. "Yes, exactly like that. It surprised me, actually."

"Obviously so," Thant observed.

Bolan ignored the interruption. "Had you ever followed them before?"

"No. It was against policy, and they know that as well as we do. They shouldn't have been expecting us, unless... unless they had some reason to know Miss May was more than a social worker. But I don't see how they could know that."

"Do you think they *were* expecting you?"

"I don't know. It's possible they always lay an ambush. There's no way to know."

"But if it wasn't their normal practice, they might have known something about Miss May that you didn't know. Isn't that right?"

Salang nodded. "Yes, that's right. But I can't be sure."

The big American stared hard at Bishop. "Well, what about it?"

"Bolan, look, I don't know what you're getting at, but—"

"What I'm getting at is that either you may not be telling us everything about Katherine May, or that Katherine May may not have told you everything about herself."

"That's not possible."

"I wouldn't bet my life on it," Bolan stated. "I want to talk to somebody in Vietnamese intelligence."

"No way."

"No deal."

"They'd never permit it."

"Ask."

"But..."

Bolan stood. "I can't speak for the lieutenant, but as far as I'm concerned, we have nothing more to discuss." He moved toward the door.

Bishop got up out of his chair. "Wait...I'll see what I can do. But I'm not making any promises."

"Your kind never does."

BOLAN'S PHONE RANG insistently. He picked it up, and the desk clerk on the other end said, "There's a Mr. Bishop here to see you."

"Send him up." Bolan cradled the receiver and stared at the phone, wondering whether Bishop was here to tell him what he wanted to hear, or if it was going to be the same kind of runaround he'd been getting.

The warrior opened the door at Bishop's brief rap and admitted the man, who looked frazzled. He tried a diplomatic smile, but Bolan wasn't buying it.

"Well?" Bolan said as he closed the door.

"You got what you wanted." Bishop didn't seem happy about it, and the Executioner waited for more. There was bound to be more. There always was.

"This isn't easy."

"It never is."

"Look, I know you're plugged in somewhere high up. I can live with that. But if you screw this up, I'll have your head."

"If I screw this up, you'll never see me again."

Bishop crossed the carpet carefully, as if it were a living thing. He dropped into a chair and let his shoulders sag. "You know, there's always some hot-shot who thinks he knows my job better than I do."

"Does he?" Bolan asked.

"Does he what?"

"Know your job better than you do?"

"You're a wise guy, aren't you?"

"Not really. But I have to tell you, Bishop, if I nad a buck for every clown in your little arm of the government who thought he knew best, I'd be a wealthy man."

"Is that what you want out of this—money?"

"You know better than that."

Bishop rubbed his face with both palms. When he spoke, his voice was muffled by his fingers. "Yeah, I do know better. Look, I don't mean to be a pain in the ass, but I've spent four years trying to piece together a little thing with the Viets. It's working, but it's held together with spit and chewing gum. If it comes apart,

I'm looking at eight years to put it back together. Do you understand what that means?"

Bolan nodded. "Look at it from my side for a minute. If I go out there blind, chances are I might not be able to do anything for you. And innocent people could get killed."

"You have to go along to get along," Bishop replied. "It's not necessary for a soldier to know everything a general knows."

"In my experience, generals know less than they think, and soldiers don't know as much as they should."

"Maybe you're right."

"No maybe about it. Now tell me the whole thing on Katherine May. I want chapter and verse."

Bishop rubbed one nervous hand across his chin and sighed deeply. "All right. The only thing I didn't tell you before, when Thant was there, was this—Katherine did this as a favor to me. She used to be one of ours, but she wanted out. She's been out of it for a few years."

"And you made her come back. Just this once—right?"

"Yeah, right. But I meant it. We lost three people recently. She knew the drill, and it was time for a run. There wasn't time to train anybody else. We'd been hearing stuff, nothing definite, but we had reason to believe the drop was critical. I didn't twist her arm. I didn't threaten her. I asked. That's all, just asked. And she said yes, and now..."

"And . . . ?"

"And what?"

"There's more, isn't there?"

"Just this. Her old man's pretty high up in some aerospace company. He's wired, Defense Department and stuff, a lot of juice. And he's pissed off. He doesn't even know his daughter used to work for us."

"Your ass is in a sling, right?"

Bishop nodded. "All the way up to my neck."

Bolan leaned forward. "Now, do I get to talk to this Viet, or don't I?"

"You get more than that. He's going with you."

"The hell he is."

"It's the only way he'll help. Take it or leave it."

"I want to talk to him first."

"Fine. He said the same thing."

"Let's go then."

The State Department honcho sighed. He rubbed his face again, like a man who had just awakened from a deep sleep and found he had a hangover he couldn't explain. Finally he nodded. "You got it."

As Bishop stepped to the door, Bolan slipped on a light jacket to cover his side arms. Then the two men left the room and walked down the hall to the elevator.

"You been to Bangkok before?" Bishop asked.

"Yeah, I have."

"Know the city?"

"Not well, but well enough."

Bishop pressed the button, then turned to Bolan. "This is the first time this man has ever met with anybody else on our side. Do me a favor and forget about the past. If you have any grudges, leave 'em here. Understood?"

Bolan didn't answer, but Bishop seemed satisfied.

In the lobby they were met by another man, whom Bishop introduced only as his driver. The car was waiting in a small VIP parking area around the side of the building. Bolan climbed into the back with Bishop, who seemed disinclined to speak.

The driver threaded his way through the heavy traffic along a broad boulevard. They were creeping along, but the man was adept at squeezing the Buick into places a lesser man might have thought too tight. Unlike the other drivers in the throng, the American refused to use his horn. He ignored shaken fists and shouted curses, regardless of the language, and kept his eyes peeled for another two- or three-yard advance.

Bolan looked out the window, then turned to look behind every so often. He didn't like the feeling of constraint—the car couldn't move more than a few yards if it had to. He watched two young men on a motor scooter, who seemed to be hanging back. It made him wonder. The little Honda would have fit easily between the trucks and vans, which was one reason they were so numerous in Bangkok.

The warrior was growing uneasy. He opened his coat and loosened the Beretta under his arm. Bishop noticed, but said nothing.

The scooter was still behind them two minutes later when Bolan turned again. The driver started to edge his way to the left, getting ready to turn into a narrow side street. The car spurted forward suddenly, leaving a huge hole in the traffic as the Buick swung around the corner.

They made fifteen or twenty yards before braking again. Bolan looked over his shoulder once more, and the Honda was still there. He debated calling it to the driver's attention, but decided against it. No point, he thought, in tipping his hand. For all he knew Bishop and the driver were aware of the Honda, perhaps even responsible for it.

He sat forward slightly and was able to pick up the Honda in the passenger side mirror. The scooter remained fifty feet behind the car. The driver of the Honda balanced the machine on one leg, gunning the engine. Over the steady noise of the crowd Bolan could hear the small engine whining like a chain saw.

The car lurched forward a few feet, and Bolan looked ahead and spotted an opening in the traffic. He leaned over the back of the front seat and told the driver to move the car into the gap.

The driver glanced over his shoulder. "You think I like this?" But he gunned the engine, and the Buick screeched ahead another twenty feet, narrowly squeezing between a pair of large vans. The Honda followed, still hanging back the same fifty feet or so.

Suddenly the scooter spurted, raising its front wheel off the ground. The passenger no longer had his arms around the driver's waist. He leaned to the left as the Honda raced toward the car.

"Down!" Bolan shouted, shoving the driver over and away from the wheel.

"What the hell are you doing?" Bishop roared.

The Executioner drew the Beretta and turned to the side window. The Honda was ten feet away now, the passenger leaning toward the car, grinning. He leveled an Uzi, and his intention was clear.

Bolan fired through the glass, but the scooter was too quick. The enemy gunner let loose a sustained burst that shattered the windows on the passenger side of the Buick. Slugs ripped at the top of the front seat and the dashboard, then blew out the windshield. Bolan kept his head low, the Beretta ready but useless in his hand.

He couldn't fire blind—there was too much of a crowd—but he couldn't raise his head to see as long as the Uzi chewed away at the car.

The driver grabbed the steering wheel and stomped on the gas pedal. It was crude but effective. The car roared backward and slammed into a van just turning the corner. Bolan shoved his door open and tumbled into the street, coming up into a crouch. The Honda was making a tight circle, the driver keeping the scooter up with one bent leg while the passenger rammed a fresh magazine into the Uzi.

Bolan dropped to one knee and fired twice, just as the scooter straightened and started toward him. His first shot slammed into the driver, knocking him off the vehicle. The impact sent the Uzi flying, and the bike started to tilt. Bolan's second shot punctured the small gas tank, sending fuel spurting onto the pavement. People had begun to scream, and they tried to run, but the narrow street was jammed. The bike went over, its exhaust scraping the asphalt. Sparks ignited the geyser of fuel.

In slow motion the flame chewed its way back toward the tank. The scooter fell and the gunner tried to scramble away, but he was tangled in the wreckage. He was on his feet now and Bolan charged toward him. The passenger had one foot caught, but it broke free just as the flames reached the tank.

It blew with a sharp crack and a muffled roar. The driver, the bike and the gunner all disappeared behind the huge fireball. Thick black smoke swirled up into the bright sky. The flames looked almost transparent under the bright sunlight.

The gunner spun like a dervish, screaming and flapping his arms, trying to put out the fuel-soaked clothing already turning to black tatters on his slender form.

Someone rushed toward him with a blanket, but the kid kept whirling away. He collapsed suddenly, like a balloon suddenly out of air, and lay there in a ball.

Bolan raced toward him, snatched the blanket and smothered the flames, but it was already too late.

Bolan could smell the sickening odor of charred flesh as he tugged the blanket away. Contorted by agony, the gunner's mouth curled in a sinister parody of a grin. But the eyes were motionless in the blackened face.

He was dead, and he wouldn't be able to tell Bolan who had contracted the hit. Or why.

The warrior turned back to the car. Bishop was helping the driver out of the front passenger door. As Bolan approached, the State man turned to him. "That was close."

Bolan wondered if it was close enough.

2

"What was that all about?" Bolan asked. Bishop, still shaken, brushed at his clothes. Slivers of glass glittered in the sunlight. Trapped in the cloth of his jacket and pants, they made him look as if he were covered with tiny jewels.

"I could ask you the same thing," Bishop replied. "Somebody obviously knew who we were and maybe where we were going."

"Maybe your man from Vietnamese intelligence isn't as trustworthy as you think," Bolan suggested.

The man from State bristled but didn't argue. Bolan had a point, and he was just as curious as the big man. "Maybe we should ask him about that," Bishop said.

"If you don't mind," the driver said, "I'd like to do the asking."

Bishop whirled. "Forget it, George. No rough stuff. The guy is still valuable, even if he sold us out."

"Valuable to whom?" George asked.

"Quit bellyaching. No harm done. And maybe he had nothing to do with it."

George gave Bishop a look of profound disbelief, but he didn't say anything. It was obvious Bishop had already made up his mind about how to handle things.

"I guess we better walk the rest of the way," Bishop said. He gave a little laugh, but no one joined him, and it died away quickly. The sound of sirens was drifting across the market quarter, but it would be several minutes before the police could work their way through the tangled traffic. The three men left the car, its engine still smoking under the hood where several slugs had chewed at the block and severed several hoses.

"You want me to stay and wait for the police?" George asked his superior.

"No. I want you with us." Bishop paused, then said, "If you're right, we're going to need you."

"If he's right," Bolan said, "your man won't be there. He doesn't really expect you, and he sure doesn't want to see you if you show up."

Bishop nodded. He looked at the crowd, still standing some distance from the steaming wreck. Terror had subsided, overcome by curiosity, and the perimeter was beginning to shrink. "Come on," he said.

The State man led the way into the throng. As the Executioner followed Bishop through the marketplace, he thought over what had happened. In less than twenty-four hours it had become apparent that there was a lot more to the situation than Bishop had told him. Perhaps more than the man himself had known.

Who *was* Katherine May, anyway? he wondered. And what did she know that would warrant a brazen assassination attempt like the one they'd so narrowly escaped? The questions whirled around, unanswered.

Half a mile later Bishop stopped in his tracks and pointed to a narrow alleyway across the jammed street. "We're here," he announced.

"Tell me about this Vietnamese," Bolan said.

"Not much to tell. Name's Kwanh Dieu Cao. Captain in the NVA during the war. At twenty-four. He's a colonel now. They're toying with the notion of asking for normalization, and they're scared shitless of China. They need us. I think Kwanh knows it, and I think he knows we know it. That's why I trust him."

"That's it?"

"That's all I'm going to tell you. The rest has nothing to do with the present situation."

"Is that what you call it when somebody tries to kill you in broad daylight? A situation?"

"Look, the man and his government aren't angels. I know that. But Pol Pot is a whole different ball game. I don't know what you know about the Khmer Rouge, but I know enough to make me toss my cookies if I think about it. And I can't help thinking about it. Not after what I've seen. Not after the stories I've heard. I wasn't always a desk jockey. I've *been* there, damn it. I've been inside Cambodia and I've seen slaughterhouses that weren't as bloody. Unless you've stood in a room full of skulls, ten thousand empty eye sockets staring at you, then you have no idea what I'm talking about. I don't ever want to have an experience like that again. Not ever."

Bishop stopped speaking. He'd broken out in a sweat, and his hands trembled as he tried to light a cigarette. Bolan waited, then when it was apparent Bishop was too shaken, he took the matchbook, ripped a match out and struck it. Bishop cupped the bigger man's hand in both of his own, leaned toward the flame and lit his cigarette. His hands continued to shake, and when he exhaled, the trembling of his lips made little clumps of smoke.

Starting to calm down, he took another long drag, let the smoke spin out in a long, thin tendril and pointed. "The man over there on the third floor knows what I'm talking about, and he's the best chance we have of getting Katherine back. If we get her back, we get a line on Pol Pot. We also get a swarm of congressional bees out of our collective bonnet. And that counts for something with my people. Understand?"

Bolan understood only too well. "Let's go talk to Kwanh."

Bishop led the way into the street, which was a nonstop din of horns and loud mufflers, interspersed with shrill whistles from the pedicab drivers and the squeak of worn brakes. On the far side Bishop paused again, waiting at the mouth of the alleyway.

"Maybe I should go myself."

Bolan shook his head. "No way. Not now."

"Look, if you think I had any—"

Bolan cut him off. "I don't think anything right now. But even if Kwanh didn't have anything to do with what happened, it's best if we stick together. They knew enough, whoever they are, to know we were coming to see him. For all you know Kwanh wasn't quite so lucky. Or they could be waiting for us."

Bishop sighed. "You're right, of course. But..." He shrugged. "I guess I just don't want to think about the implications."

"I don't want to think about anything *but* the implications."

At the back end of the alley, Bishop posted George as a rear guard, then led the way up a rickety flight of wooden steps. On a small landing at the top he rapped on a door, his knuckles knocking curls of peeling paint loose.

No one answered the door, so he rapped again, this time harder. Bolan heard a thud inside, then a scrape. Footsteps approached the door, and he rested his hand inside his jacket, curled around the butt of his Beretta.

The doorknob rattled, then turned with a squeal of reluctant metal as the door swung inward. A small man, obviously Vietnamese, stood just inside, blinking at the bright sunlight. Bolan could see past the man's shoulders into a dimly lit room. As far as he could tell, the guy was alone.

The Vietnamese stepped back and bowed, sweeping the floor with his fingertips as he ushered Bishop then Bolan through the door. He closed it quickly. There was a thud in the next room, and Bolan fisted the Beretta in a flash.

Kwanh flinched but made no other move. He smiled. "I see your friend is nervous, Clayton. I understand."

"I don't think you do," Bishop replied.

"Yes, he does," Bolan said. "News travels fast in Bangkok. Especially that kind of news." He holstered the pistol.

The smile broadened. "You're not just big, are you? Kwanh Dieu Cao," he said, sticking out a hand. "And you are . . . ?"

Bolan accepted the hand out of courtesy, but declined to give his name. It had no effect on the smile.

"I understand you killed those responsible for the attack," Kwanh commented. "That's unfortunate."

"Not those responsible," Bishop clarified. "Only those who attempted it. They weren't acting on their own."

"Of course not. And do you have any idea who might have been behind it?"

"No."

Kwanh nodded, the smile disappearing. "Your friend, I think, believes I might have had something to do with it."

"No, he doesn't. He's just—"

Kwanh held up a hand. "The man should speak for himself." He looked squarely at Bolan, his dark eyes glittering.

Bolan nodded. "I can't see any reason why you should be ruled out."

"Nor do I, except for the fact that I'm not in any way involved. I don't blame you for being suspicious, though."

Kwanh turned to lead the way into the back room. Bolan followed Bishop, relaxing a bit but still vigilant.

The room was small. Bookshelves occupied three of the walls. Books were crammed into the shelves, and magazines hung at odd angles where they'd been jammed into every available cranny. A small table in one corner sported a computer, and paper was everywhere.

Kwanh sat behind his desk, then motioned his visitors to a pair of chairs. Bishop accepted but stayed poised on the front edge of the seat. Bolan elected to stand.

The Vietnamese stared at the two Americans, his face impassive. Bolan watched him closely. Finally, leaning back in his chair, Kwanh nodded his head.

"All right," he said. "We're already behind. Maybe we can catch up, and maybe not. But I must insist on two things before we do anything at all."

"What?" Bishop asked.

"Absolute candor, first."

"Of course. What else?"

"Absolute secrecy. Total. It's absolutely imperative that no one outside your government know about our cooperation, and even those who do should be few in number. As few as possible."

"I understand." Bishop turned to look over his shoulder at Bolan. The big man made no move. "That's agreeable to you, isn't it?"

"What about the Thai government?" Bolan asked.

Kwanh thought about it as if it hadn't occurred to him before. But Bolan was sure it had. "I'll take care of that end," the Viet replied.

"Okay." Bolan shifted his weight but remained standing, his arms folded across his chest. "What do you know about the attack?"

"Maybe a great deal, maybe nothing."

"Either you do or you don't."

"I'll know for certain later this evening," Kwanh told him.

"Then suppose you tell us what you *do* know."

"I can give you an outline. The rest of the details I can fill in later."

"Later? When? You said yourself that we were already playing catch-up. There's no time for later."

"But," Kwanh said, the smile returning more brilliant than ever, "since I'm going with you, we have all the time in the world."

KATHERINE MAY SAT in the darkest corner of the hut, which stank of spices and human waste. Her hand touched something damp on the floor, and she pulled it away, wiping the mush on the thatched walls, afraid of what it might be. She was exhausted after two days of forced march. Seven people had died on the way, left to rot like fallen trees. Swirling emotions had her nerves on edge, and she wondered if she was too long removed from this world to survive.

She listened to the babel of voices outside. She'd tried to pick up scraps of conversation during the march, but the Khmer Rouge guerrillas were careful around their prisoners. One man kept watching her, as if trying to place her, but the rest paid no attention to her whatsoever.

She'd mixed in with the refugees, wanting to be as anonymous as possible. It had been foolish of her to challenge the guerrillas, and she could kick herself for her stupidity. But it was too late for that. All she could do now was to bide her time.

And try to stay alive.

The guerrillas had been almost cavalier in their treatment of their captives. They hadn't bothered to search her, and she was grateful for that. The small Browning automatic in her pocket gave her some comfort. It was only a .32, and she had one spare clip. Eighteen bullets wasn't much, but it was a lifeline, and she clung to it.

But Katherine knew, too, that they'd eventually get around to questioning her. She'd made the mistake of calling attention to herself at Chulingorn and, sooner or later, someone would wonder why. When that moment came, they'd come for her. She had to do something with the gun. If they found it on her, she'd lose it, and maybe her life. But if she left it in the hut, she might never get back to it.

It was a Hobson's choice. Discovery was almost a certainty, and she had to avoid it at all cost. She slipped the gun out of her pocket and groped along the wall of the hut. The thick branches and matlike fronds offered a thousand nooks where she might hide it, but she wanted to make sure she could get to it in a hurry if she had to. If she needed a gun, she wasn't likely to have time to play touchy-feely with the wall.

Directly across from the low doorway, she found a pole, but there was no place to deposit the pistol because the thatching was too snug. Cautiously she got to her feet and walked toward the doorway.

A rough lintel, still showing the stubs where branches had been lopped off close to the bark of the thick trunk, ran the width of the doorway. It wasn't thick enough to serve as a ledge, but there was a shallow depression behind it. She stuck her fingers in and wiggled them, widening the opening just enough to accept the pistol.

The gun slid in, and she drew the extra clip out of her back pocket, dropped it next to the Browning and backed away. She crossed the hut and sat down again, staring at the lintel. Light seeped in through the cracks around the door to the hut. It hurt her eyes, and when she closed them, she saw the lines etched on her retinas.

Sitting there, Katherine started to feel more like a caged animal than a human being. She'd forgotten what life was like, even in the best of times, in this part of the world. She'd tried so hard to get away from it and, when she succeeded, to forget about it altogether. Even her work with the council, and the constant exposure to the misery and deprivation, hadn't brought it back this forcefully. She'd wondered why for two days, and now the answer was plain. Then she'd been above it. It had been apart from her. She was an outsider. Now she was at its mercy once more, and her ability to endure would be tested to its limit. And perhaps beyond.

Here she was, right back where she started. The camp had done it, she thought, unhinged her somehow. Seeing all those people jammed together and smelling the awful stench of concentrated poverty had made her snap.

Or maybe it was just as her father had said. Maybe she never had control of her feelings. Maybe she let circumstances get the best of her. And the thought of her father made her eyes fill. She heard a whimper and snapped her head around, looking into the darkest recesses of the hut. She strained to see in the dark but could see only the faint seepage of light through the thatch. When she convinced herself she was alone in the hut, she was forced to admit the whimper had been hers. Choked out of her by her rage and embarrassment, she had disowned it, refused to admit it had come from her own throat.

But it had.

She was on the edge of losing it altogether. She felt her composure slipping away a little bit at a time. It would only be a matter of time before she would be reduced to trembling jelly.

She had to get out of this place. It would be better to take her chances in the jungle on her own than to stay. She wondered if anyone was looking for her. The lieutenant had seemed competent. He'd been a little distant at first, but he knew what he was doing. Maybe he was looking for her right now.

She kept thinking of Trang. He was Vietnamese, and yet he had tried to help. Maybe he had his own reasons, but in the long run it wouldn't matter. What was good for Cambodia was good for Cambodia, regardless of who wanted it or why. She wondered where Trang was now. Would he get word to his superiors? Could they help her? Would they care enough?

Katherine wished that she'd found him, had had time to talk to him. It couldn't be helped, but all she had was sketches, broad outlines, the meager bits Clayton Bishop had told her. They were frightening and they were suggestive, but they weren't concrete. There was nothing she could do about it, and what she did know might very well die with her. Unless she got lucky. But she hadn't been so far, and there was nothing to suggest her luck was about to change.

She walked to the door and listened. The voices still carried from outside, but they were so far away that she couldn't make out the words. She wondered whether she'd be interrogated. Did they have a reason?

But she knew the answer to that. Her conduct had been so bizarre that they might want to try to find out why she'd behaved as she had. Or they might conclude that she was a lunatic. That wouldn't be any better—maybe worse.

She heard footsteps approaching, and two men talking in lowered voices. The steps slowed as they got closer, as if the men were trying to finish a private conversation before reaching the hut. One of them laughed, and then the footsteps picked up again.

Katherine backed away from the door, halfway across the hut, reaching behind her to feel for the wall. She didn't get that far before the door was thrown open. A man stood framed in the doorway, his arms folded behind his back. She'd seen men do this before, the posture of studied arrogance. Teachers used it to intimidate rebellious students. Her professors in college had done the same thing. And policemen. Which one of those things was this man in the doorway? she wondered.

Then, realizing where she was, she knew he couldn't be a teacher or a professor. Those people had all been killed, bullets emptying their brains of everything they'd tried so hard to learn.

She remembered the worst days of the terror, when people threw away their glasses and burned their books. Intellectuals suddenly forgot the alphabet, the literate lost the ability to read. To know anything was to know only that you were certain to die. Was it still that way?

Of course it was, she told herself. Pol Pot still walked the earth. His ideas would be here at least as long as the man himself. She thought about the reading glasses in her bag. But it was too late to hide them now. Perhaps she could leave the bag.

She slipped it off her shoulder and let it slide down the back of her leg. She crossed her fingers, hoping it was too dark for the man in the doorway to have seen the gesture. She felt foolish, a kid caught wearing her mother's makeup. She realized the gears weren't quite meshing in her head.

Then, as if he had been waiting for her to divest herself of the bag, the man stepped into the hut. His boots squished on the damp ground, their leather squeaking like rusty hinges as he stepped slowly and purposefully toward her. She remembered the Uncle Ho sandals the Khmer Rouge had worn and wondered what had happened to them, where the boots had come from. The man's hands were still behind his back, and his hips pivoted in an exaggerated motion. Like transvestites in Amsterdam, she thought. It almost made her giggle, but she suppressed the urge and chewed at her lower lip.

This was no laughing matter. This man might blow a hole in her skull for no other reason than that he felt like it, or that he hadn't blown a hole in anyone's skull for several days and it was time for a fix.

The man planted himself directly in front of her. She realized he'd been waiting for his eyes to adjust to the gloom. Since the light was behind him, she couldn't see his face. He seemed to be a thick slab of shadow in squeaky leather boots, just standing there in front of her.

The man remained silent. Even in the darkness she had the distinct sensation that his eyes were boring into her. Her cheeks grew hot and her temper started to flare. But she had to be patient. If she lost control of herself, the consequences might just be fatal. The man shifted his weight slightly. His boots made a sucking sound in the damp earth.

Then he turned and strode back through the doorway and into the sunlight. Katherine let her breath out slowly, reluctant to believe that she'd gotten off so easily, at least for the time being. The man muttered something in Khmer, his accent rough and unpolished, the speech of a peasant.

Immediately a second man appeared in the doorway.

His use of Khmer was no more skillful. "Come with me," he ordered, then stepped aside to wait for her.

Slowly she approached the open doorway. She could see this man clearly. The light was so bright that it washed out his features a bit and spread dark shadows under his eyes and nose, his prominent lower lip shading his chin. He was young, perhaps twenty, certainly no older.

She stood in the doorway for a long moment, like a diver at the edge of the board watching the water fifty feet below. She took a deep breath. The first step was the hardest. When she was outside, she felt the heat of the sun on her dark shirt and khaki pants. It felt good, as if it were killing whatever diseases lurked in the dark.

The man turned abruptly and marched across the open compound.

Katherine had no choice but to follow him.

Bodorn Salang glanced past Bolan at the small man standing behind him. The lieutenant wrinkled his nose, and his face assumed a puzzled look. He waited for the big American to introduce his companion, and when an introduction wasn't forthcoming, he pointed. "Is he coming with us?"

Bolan nodded. "Yes."

"Then we better go. We want to get there and back before dark. I don't like the thought of going into the jungle as it is. After the sun sets, I'll like it even less." He jerked a thumb into the air, and the pilot, who'd been watching him closely, cranked up the chopper. The drooping blades of the rotor began to shudder as the powerful engine made its presence felt throughout the body of the Huey. The blades started to move now, sporadically for a few seconds, then settling into a steady motion.

Bolan climbed into the cabin and waited for Salang to join him. Kwanh was the last man aboard. He looked frightened, which surprised Bolan. Then he remembered what the helicopter had been in the Vietnam War—a mechanized vulture spouting fire and brimstone over all of Indochina. To Kwanh it must have been a nightmarish sight.

When the rotor was up to speed, the pilot opened the throttle and the helicopter started to shake. Slowly it lifted off the ground a few yards and slipped sideways. It spun in a wide one-eighty, then climbed straight up. Kwanh held on to the bench. Bolan noticed the man's white knuckles. He thought about reassuring the colonel, but decided it might be more embarrassing if he called attention to the man's obvious terror.

The base fell away below them, the chopper tilted forward, and they were out over the jungle canopy. The pilot brought his machine up another thousand. Bolan guessed they were about twenty-five hundred feet in the air. The engine was running a little rough, and he could feel tremors under his feet as the Huey struggled.

Kwanh, too, was aware of the shuddering floor, and he looked even tenser than previously. Bolan leaned toward him. "Shall I introduce you now?"

The Vietnamese, grateful for the chance to think about anything but the imminent crash of the big chopper, nodded. Bolan motioned to Salang to come closer. The Thai took a seat between the two men, and Bolan performed the amenities. Salang stiffened just a bit when he heard the name. Bolan realized the Thais were no more enamored of the Vietnamese than the Chinese were. It seemed as if everybody in Southern Asia hated everyone else.

But every country had its own agenda, which meant doing whatever you had to do to look out for yourself. Eat with the devil if you had to; just make sure somebody tastes the food first.

Kwanh watched the Thai lieutenant with suspicion, as if he thought Salang might try to hurl him from the aircraft. Bolan was aware of the look, and of the mistrust it represented. Then it hit him. He remembered all the stories, not a few of them true, about VCs being taken up in choppers and held out the door by the heels until they were ready to talk. If they weren't ready, they came down a lot quicker than they'd gone up. Sometimes that was so even if they did talk.

Kwanh wouldn't be unaware of that ugly little wrinkle during the war. Bolan reached behind Salang and tapped the Viet on the shoulder. "Tell Lieutenant Salang what you told me yesterday."

Kwanh hesitated for a moment, then nodded. He started to talk, and Bolan stood and walked to the open door, watching the jungle slide by beneath them. They had an hour before they would reach Chulingorn, and Bolan needed some time to piece things together. He felt as if he were caught between the stones of a mill. There was a lot of deep-seated hatred here. He knew but hadn't lived the history of the region. No amount of study could bring him the depth of the passions that made the two men behind him what they were.

And now they were heading toward a gray zone where those passions were raw and real, like open sores. The hostility of the Vietnamese was a reality he would have to deal with.

He looked to the north, where the blue sky grew a little darker, almost like a faint line of shadow where the sky met the jungle. Beyond that line, he knew, lay China, the biggest puzzle of them all. And a part of that puzzle was the role of the Chinese in the current situation. And it was no small part.

Kwanh had told him much, and asked as many questions, all rhetorical, as Bolan himself. There was much that neither man knew, and somewhere out there was a woman who, perhaps, knew a little more than either of them. But where was she? And was she still alive?

When Bolan turned back, the two men were still talking. Kwanh seemed to have gotten a grip on his terror, Salang to have overcome his initial animosity. The lieutenant was absorbed in the briefing. He must have felt Bolan's eyes on him, because he glanced up and waved the warrior over.

"This is much more complicated than I thought," he said.

Bolan sighed. "It always is."

"We can talk more later," Kwanh said. "How long to the camp?"

"Fifteen minutes, maybe twenty," Salang replied. "No more than that."

"And you're sure Cambodians took Miss May?"

Salang nodded. "Who else could they have been?"

The question hung in the air for a long moment. Neither Kwanh nor Bolan wanted to answer it. They didn't have to. It dawned on Salang suddenly, and he shook his head. "No, they weren't Chinese. I know that."

"None of them?" Kwanh asked.

"None that I saw. Why do you think they might have been?"

"Because the Chinese want to keep a foothold in Cambodia. They're the ones who are supplying the Khmer Rouge with arms. Some food, too, though not enough. That's why they come and abduct their own people from your camps."

The three men sat quietly for several minutes. When they were over the camp, Bolan walked back to the open door and looked down at the tent city, which sprawled like an ugly stain on the riverbank. The water of a tributary of the Mun River, swollen with recent rain, its muddy brown turned to a creamy beige by turbulence, swept away in a long, wandering arc.

Salang joined him at the door.

"Show me where the ambush occurred," Bolan said.

Salang barked into the cabin mike, and the chopper swerved. Directly below Bolan could see a road. The pilot dropped lower and followed the narrow ribbon of space through the dense forest.

Salang seemed to be looking for something, perhaps a landmark. He pointed northward at a low mountain and directed the pilot to change course.

"There," he said, "near the foot of that mountain. That's where—"

He didn't finish, and Bolan couldn't blame him. It always hurt to remember losing a friend. Salang had lost eleven that day. The man was lucky to be alive, and he knew it. But he had that guilt that made surviving so much harder to bear than it should be.

"But there was no camp there?" Bolan asked.

Kwanh joined them, standing with his back to the cabin wall and both hands locked on the safety rail. He tried to look out but couldn't force himself.

Bolan was about to say something when the squawkbox crackled. Salang jerked his head around and leaned out to look at the road. He pointed, and the warrior peered over the edge. Far below, and more than a mile ahead, a small figure stumbled along a rutted roadway. Salang told the pilot to drop down to fifty feet, and the chopper descended for a few seconds.

They closed on the figure quickly. A handful of men had suddenly spilled into the road. They spotted the stumbling figure nearly five hundred yards ahead of them. They saw the chopper, too, and started to run.

Bolan had expected them to dash back into the jungle, but they ran toward their quarry. The Executioner could tell it was a woman now, and for a moment he thought it might be Katherine May. But even as the thought crossed his mind, he knew it couldn't be that easy.

The woman fell, got to her feet again, then tripped and fell to her knees. The men were closing fast, and Bolan clicked the safety off his M-16.

"What are you doing?" Salang demanded.

Bolan ignored him and raised the rifle as the chopper fishtailed slightly.

"What are you doing?" the lieutenant repeated, this time reaching out for the rifle. "You don't even know who those men are. You can't just shoot them."

"I don't plan to shoot them. But I don't intend to watch them shoot the woman, either."

The words were no sooner out of his mouth than several little spouts of dust erupted around the woman. She'd fallen forward now, doubled over her knees. The thunder of the chopper engine drowned out the gunshots, but there was no doubt the men had fired at the woman.

Bolan cut loose with a short burst. Firing at long range, with the chopper drifting, he just wanted to keep the men back. He saw them scatter, one pointing at the chopper as if they were aware of it for the first time. He wondered why.

"Tell the pilot to land," Bolan shouted.

Salang stared at him, and the warrior shoved him toward the intercom mike.

The chopper drifted forward then began its descent. They were ten feet off the ground now, and the small band of men was still coming on. At touchdown Bolan sprang from the Huey and raced toward the woman. She was still hunched over, but the Executioner couldn't see any blood. As far as he could tell, she hadn't been shot.

Bullets whined past him as he grabbed the woman around the waist. Kwanh jumped to the ground and knelt beside the chopper, cutting loose with short, sharp bursts that stopped the charging men in their tracks.

Bolan hoisted the woman off the ground, stunned by how little she weighed. Bracing the frail body against his hip, he sprinted back toward the helicopter. Salang leaned out and helped the woman inside.

The warrior tapped Kwanh and covered the man as he climbed into the Huey. The men on the ground, furious at having lost their prey, emptied their magazines. Bullets clanged off the chopper and ripped at the ground around its skids as Bolan tumbled back into the cabin.

The woman rolled onto her back as the warrior knelt over her. He looked at Salang, more to confirm that it wasn't Katherine May than anything else. The lieutenant shook his head.

The chopper lifted off, and Bolan watched the ground fall away. The men were already gone.

And he was more in the dark than ever. But maybe the woman would change all that.

Maybe.

SALANG LOOKED at Bolan quietly. He was trying to size up the big American, but he couldn't get a fix on him. The man was not so much distant as self-contained. He had an assurance about him that Salang envied. The American unnerved him.

He turned his attention to the smaller man. Kwanh was unnerving, too. The immobile face made his small size seem somehow threatening. It was like looking at a bomb and wondering when it would go off.

He cursed the bad fortune that had brought him to this point, but the curse did nothing to change it. He heaved a sigh.

"According to the woman, there's a small camp of Khmer Rouge about three kilometers from the spot where we picked her up. She says it isn't a work camp, just a military camp, maybe thirty soldiers. The work camp's much deeper inside Cambodia. She escaped from the work camp two weeks ago."

"Does she know anything about Katherine May?" Bolan asked.

"Maybe. She says they have a special prisoner, a woman. She didn't know her name and she never saw her, only heard talk from some of the other inmates of the camp. There are more Khmer Rouge there, maybe a hundred. She's not sure because it changes all the time."

"We have to assume May's being held there," Bolan said. "There's no other place to start."

"I have a small unit, handpicked men," Salang told him, "but there will be no support from the army. Once we go in we're on our own."

"When do we leave?"

"One hour."

Kwanh got to his feet and started to pace. "No support. Does that mean no supplies?"

"No supplies other than what we take with us," Salang replied.

"We could be gone for a month, maybe two."

Salang laughed. "We won't last that long. If we aren't out in a week, we won't be coming out at all. I've requisitioned enough ammunition and food for two weeks. We'll have three jeeps for the first part of the operation. After that we'll have to move on foot. There are few roads worthy of the name in that corner of Cambodia, so it hardly matters."

"Air support?" Kwanh asked.

"We'll have radio contact. We can request helicopter pickup, provided we're no more than one hundred kilometers across the border. Any more than that and they won't come for us."

Bishop had sat quietly in the corner. His face was shrouded in shadow, and Bolan wondered what he was thinking. When it was obvious that Salang was finished with the briefing, Bishop got to his feet and pulled Bolan aside. "You understand that you're completely on your own out there, don't you?"

Bolan nodded. "Yeah, I understand that."

"Except for one thing," Bishop said.

"What's that?"

"Here, take this." He thrust a small book into Bolan's hand. "A code book. If you need some air cover, or if you need a helo pickup, you got it. One time only on the air cover, though, so don't waste it. It could get pretty hairy out there, but we want Katherine May back. Very badly."

Bolan was quiet for a long time. Finally he said, "Bishop, I want you to know one thing. If you're holding out on me, I'll come back for you. Count on it."

Bishop extended a hand. "Good luck. You're going to need it."

It was time to go. Salang escorted Bishop to the door, then closed it. "If either of you wants anything in particular in the way of weapons, now's the time to tell me. Otherwise . . ." He shrugged.

When neither man spoke, Salang led them down to a waiting jeep. They rode in silence. Bolan was thinking about what lay ahead, and wondering about the two men with him. Each had an ax or two to grind. He only hoped they could work together for as long as it took. Their survival, and possibly his, depended on it.

The men Salang had chosen were waiting at a warehouse at one end of the base. According to the young lieutenant, they were all combat veterans, all had been into Cambodia more than once, and each was a graduate of special training schools either at Quantico or Camp Lejeune. Their equipment was already stowed in one of the five jeeps to be used for the initial leg of the mission. Helicopters would have been better, but they were too noisy.

Surprise was a key element in the operational plan, and Bolan knew only too well how fragile an ally it was. They were fortunate that the Khmer Rouge had no air power, either for surveillance or combat support. The Chinese had been supplying guns and ammunition, as well as advisers, but no heavy equipment. But they knew the terrain, and they had everyone scared to death. If the small unit were spotted, the Khmer Rouge would know about it in a matter of hours, if not minutes.

As the jeeps rolled out through the gates, Salang looked around, like a man uncertain whether he would ever see the place again. The small convoy moved slowly, the vehicles well spaced to minimize the danger from an ambush. The sun was directly overhead, and it was getting hotter. It was already nearly a hundred degrees, and the air was thick enough to swim in.

The lead jeep suddenly slowed, then stopped. Bolan was in the third jeep, and when it halted, he stood up. Salang left his seat in the front and sprinted forward.

"What's happening?" Kwanh asked.

"Can't tell," Bolan answered. "Looks like they found something." He jumped from the jeep and ran toward the front of the small column.

Salang was in conference with two of his men, and they were pointing to a spot on the road. To Bolan's eye it looked as if the ground had been disturbed and some effort had been made to conceal the disturbance.

The lieutenant nodded, then waited while one of the men sprinted back to the lead jeep. He returned a moment later, carrying a mine detector.

"Trouble?" Bolan asked.

"Not sure. Maybe a mine," Salang replied. "And if there's one, there'll be more." He turned to watch the soldier fiddle with dials on the handle of the detector, then start a slow walk forward, waving the device from side to side.

When the soldier approached the scuff marks on the road, Bolan heard a sharp chirp, then another. The soldier took another step, and this time the detector started to chirp steadily.

"Damn!" Salang swore. "This will slow us down even more. If they're magnetic, we have a real problem. If they're pressure sensitive, we can flag them and work our way around them."

"And if they're command-detonated?" Bolan asked.

Salang looked at him sharply. "I hadn't thought of that." He barked at the man with the detector, and the soldier turned to look at his superior. He took a step back, then started to swing the detector around. There was a loud clap of thunder, and a huge geyser of earth shot into the air.

The soldier was knocked off his feet, and the detector went flying. At the same instant a flurry of gunfire erupted to the left. The soldier with the detector lay stunned, and Salang rushed toward him as bullets ripped clods of earth from the road just behind him.

The commandos spilled out of the jeeps and took up positions behind their vehicles. Bolan ran to help Salang. The soldier was unconscious but seemed otherwise unhurt. He had narrowly escaped being blown to pieces.

Bolan and Salang hauled him back to the lead jeep and put him in the back seat. The Thais had begun to return fire, and the hidden gunmen seemed to have vanished.

Salang called a cease-fire. His men stopped shooting, and the jungle suddenly fell silent. The lieutenant checked the line. One of his men had sustained a minor wound, but that was the extent of the damage.

Working his way back to Bolan, he dropped to one knee. "I don't like it. They don't usually give up so easily."

"Let's take it to them, then," Bolan suggested.

Salang shook his head slowly. "We have no choice. But if they surround us in the jungle, they'll shoot us to pieces."

"If they set up another ambush, they might shoot us to pieces, anyway. They know we're here. What have we got to lose?"

The lieutenant barked orders, splitting his unit in two. Half was to remain to guard the jeeps, the other to accompany him and Bolan. Kwanh, too, wanted to join the hunt. They were working smoothly, but with an undercurrent of frenzy. Each man knew the peril that lay ahead—death could be waiting behind the next tree, or the next.

But to a man they also knew that if word of their expedition got back to the main command post, death would be a certainty. As they eased into the jungle, Salang took the point. Bolan watched him from two posts back. He was beginning to revise his estimate of the young lieutenant. The man had courage. Like soldiers everywhere, he was trapped in a set of political rules that didn't make any sense, that tied one hand behind his back and often left the other grasping at thin air.

The attackers had dissolved, leaving not a single sign that they'd been there. A trail of sorts existed, but Bolan knew it was risky to use it. Speed was paramount, particularly chasing someone who had the advantage of intimate knowledge of the terrain. But hacking at the thick undergrowth would guarantee that the other side knew they were coming. They had no real choice; they took the trail.

Salang was moving swiftly, his head swiveling back and forth, aware it seemed of the tiniest movement of a leaf. He stopped abruptly at one point and bent down. Bolan sprinted past the two men ahead of him to join the lieutenant. "What is it?"

Salang pointed at a fine, almost transparent filament.

"Fishing line?"

Salang nodded. He grasped the line gently and squeezed it between thumbs and forefingers, leaving two inches of clear line between his hands. "It might be nothing, just something to slow us down. But cut it. . . .''

Bolan took a knife from his web belt and pressed the blade against the filament. Salang tugged his hands away from the center to make sure the pressure of the knife didn't increase tension on the line. When the blade had cut it through, he told Bolan to back away.

''Sometimes, they rig the mines to go when the line is slack,'' he said through gritted teeth. ''But not usually.''

Bolan did as he was told. When he was clear, he nodded, and Salang relaxed the tension on one end. The Executioner held his breath.

Nothing happened.

Salang relaxed the other half and sighed heavily. Backing away from the point, he rooted in the undergrowth for a heavy piece of wood. He tossed the slab a couple of feet past the limp ends of the severed filament. Instantly a geyser of earth and leaf mulch spewed up into the trees. The loud clap of the explosion made Bolan's ears ring.

When quiet returned, Salang explained, ''Sometimes the line is a decoy. When you cut it, you think you're all right. You never know what hits you when you step on the mine.''

''Yeah, I saw a lot of this in Nam.''

''We all did.''

4

The jungle closed around them again, the crater from the detonated mine yawning behind them in the center of the trail. As before, Salang took the point. This time Bolan was right behind him. The lieutenant was worried about the six men left behind to guard the supplies and the jeeps, and an undercurrent of anxiety ran through the rest as they plodded along behind Bolan.

Bolan understood Salang's reluctance, but they were too vulnerable as it was. They couldn't take the risk of getting cut off. They had to catch the ambushers before they got back to camp. If they were able to summon help, Bolan's team might be overwhelmed. One of Salang's men carried a radio sweep monitor. So far there had been no radio communication from the ambushers. If they could be caught quickly, there was a chance.

The dense undergrowth made progress slow. Salang had reconsidered the wisdom of using the trail, and angled deeper into the undergrowth. Their movement had slowed to a crawl as the lieutenant hacked at the bush with a machete, his shirt soaked through. The ground was rising gently, and Bolan knew they were climbing toward the mountain he'd seen from the air the day before.

The ambushers had been in a hurry, and in the brief stretch of trail past the booby trap, they'd made little attempt to cover their tracks. Whether because they hadn't expected to be followed, or because they knew they had the advantage, Bolan couldn't decide.

They were running parallel to the trail now. The Thai commandos were grumbling, but Salang refused to use it. Instead, he cut a swath twenty yards to the right. Every so often he'd halt the team and move out to the trail to listen.

So far he'd heard nothing. But there was still evidence of recent traffic. Even Bolan was getting impatient. He knew Salang was right about the trail, but if the Khmer Rouge were running for home, they were going to get there well before their pursuers. He thought about calling for the air cover Bishop had promised, but remembered that he had it one time only. To play that ace so soon might cost him later on. Better to bite the bullet this time, no matter how unappetizing it proved.

Suddenly the jungle seemed to come alive. Birds rose in clouds and monkeys started screeching as they swarmed through the trees, rushing toward the tiny patrol. A moment later gunfire erupted ahead of them. Salang stopped in his tracks and looked at Bolan, his face confused.

The lieutenant held up his hand, and the column stopped. He instructed his men to wait, then grabbed Bolan by the arm. "Come on. Let's see what's going on."

Salang tucked the machete back into its sheath and slipped into the brush, Bolan right behind him. The gunfire continued, but it was more sporadic now, short bursts instead of a sustained wave. The warrior ran through a number of options, but none of them made sense.

Progress was more difficult. Vines and thorny tendrils tugged at their clothes as the two men skirted the thicker patches of undergrowth. The gunfire continued to lessen in intensity, slowly dwindling away until only an occasional single shot broke the silence. By the time they covered another fifty yards the silence was again complete.

Salang dropped onto his stomach and started to worm his way along the jungle floor, ducking under the thicker branches and curling through clumps of thick, rubbery fronds.

Bolan moved to the left and picked up his pace. He was abreast of Salang now, ten yards away. The birds had settled back and the monkeys, their terror spent, had fallen quiet. Bolan could hear his own breathing now, and the scrape of cloth on vegetation. Once, a twig snapped, and he froze.

He heard Salang gasp, and turned his head. The lieutenant had found a body. Bolan crept toward him, Salang keeping his eyes glued on the corpse until the warrior placed a hand on his shoulder. The lieutenant turned and mouthed the words "Khmer Rouge."

The dead man lay on his back. He'd been shot several times, and bugs had already begun to swarm around the body, crawling up over the arms to get at the sticky front of the man's shirt.

Bolan was no stranger to death, but it still gave him pause. The insects moved in so quickly that it made him aware of just how precarious a thing life was, and just how insignificant a thing a single human being was.

For Salang it was even more threatening. The lieutenant swallowed hard, keeping his eyes averted now, locking them on Bolan's face. It was as if he were waiting for the answer to a question he'd forgotten to ask. But it didn't matter. Bolan already knew the question, and he knew, too, that he didn't know the answer.

The warrior pointed ahead. Salang nodded and, giving the corpse a wide berth, crawled to the left. Bolan circled the body on the right. They moved on another eighteen or twenty yards before they found the next body, and the third. Also Khmer Rouge.

The men had been shot in the back, running from something that still lay ahead. But what?

They proceeded another twenty yards, angling toward the trail. They had to find out what had happened, but they also had to be in a position to run if necessary. That meant risking the trail and the possibility of booby traps. It was a known risk, much better than the unknown.

They found another body, this one lying just off the trail. This man, too, had been shot in the back, obviously on the run. Bolan stopped at the edge of the trail and listened for several minutes. The jungle remained quiet.

Signaling to Salang to wait, Bolan counted to ten, then darted across the trail and into the brush. The trail veered away to the right, and he could only see ten or twelve yards before the jungle swallowed the narrow tunnel through the underbrush. He stepped out into the open, bent slightly at the waist and took a few steps, his eyes sweeping the ground carefully before he moved. There were a few scuff marks, a couple of gouges kicked in the damp mulch by running feet, but nothing else.

He remembered the trip wires in Vietnam, and the nearly invisible filament across this very trail. Salang was behind him, following in his footsteps.

The mental arithmetic was approximate. They'd found four bodies, but there had been at least twice that number firing on the small convoy. That meant at least four more Khmer Rouge were somewhere ahead of them. But were they alive or dead?

Bolan edged forward, skirting the edge of the brush. When he reached a point where he could peer around the bend in the trail, he dropped to his knees, flattened out on his stomach and crawled the last few feet.

He heard a noise to his right, swept some fronds aside with his arm, but could see nothing but more jungle.

Above, a solitary monkey barked once, then again. The small animal jumped from limb to limb, then swung out over the trail and let go, dropping a few feet to an overhanging branch from the other side of the trail. If the monkeys were coming back, the threat must be over, he thought. He crept another couple of feet.

Cocking his head toward the jungle, he listened for the sounds of flight, frightened men barreling through the undergrowth, but there was nothing. Bolan got to his feet. Holding up a hand for Salang to wait, he walked onto the trail, then finished the turn, and found the rest of the men.

Six bodies sprawled across the trail. He moved cautiously, his M-16 on full-auto, and knelt by the first corpse. One by one he checked the bodies—all had been ripped from throat to gut by gunfire from the jungle. They'd been ambushed. These six must have been downed in the first onslaught. The others managed to run some distance, but they, too, had been tracked down.

By whom? And why?

He checked the weapons and found that all six carried Chinese-made Kalashnikov assault rifles. Straightening up, he moved back around the bend to tell Salang what he'd found. The lieutenant looked puzzled.

"Who?"

Bolan shrugged. "I don't know, but it makes our job tougher. There's somebody else out here."

"What do we do now?"

"Go back and pick up the jeeps," Bolan replied. "There's nothing else we can do."

"I think we should go back."

"Back where?"

"To Thailand."

Bolan shook his head. "Not without Katherine May."

Salang stared at him. "You're mad. What could the woman know? What could be so important?"

"When we find her, I guess she'll tell us."

"We'll never find her. Not out here."

"Yes, I will," Bolan vowed.

Salang nodded, giving in.

"We might as well save time and take the trail back," Bolan suggested.

Salang agreed, and Bolan led the way. He sensed that something had changed in his relationship with the lieutenant. Without either man having said anything directly, Salang had ceded command to the American. It would make things easier for both of them. It hadn't been an easy thing for the lieutenant, and Bolan knew it. His respect for the man had grown another notch.

When they rejoined Kwanh, a check with the radioman revealed that there had been no radio contact. Bolan thought about that for a minute. It seemed significant, but he couldn't quite put his finger on the reason.

But at least it meant that the larger Khmer Rouge force was probably still unaware of their presence—if they'd ever been unaware. There was still the unsettling matter of the ambush, which wasn't easy to explain.

Bolan turned to the Vietnamese. "Kwanh, when you were here before were the Khmer Rouge in the habit of setting ambushes?"

"Always."

"Even when they had no reason to expect anyone?"

Kwanh paused. After a long silence, he nodded slightly. "I see what you're asking. No. When they expected an attack, of course. They learned that from us." There was a hint of pride in his voice. "It was an effective tactic, as you Americans learned to your sorrow. But this—" he swept his palms out in a gesture of helplessness "—makes no sense."

"So they were expecting us."

"It would seem so, yes. Or whoever turned the tables on them."

That possibility hung in the air like an invisible cloud. Bolan let it hang for a minute, then asked, "This man of yours, the one Katherine May was supposed to contact."

"What about him?"

"Could he have been turned?"

"I don't think so."

"Are you sure?"

Kwanh smiled. "No one who has lived the life I have would be sure of anything."

KWANH LOOKED WORRIED. Bolan noticed the way he kept looking around, as if he expected something to happen, or were waiting for someone. An ordinary man would be expected to show some apprehension under the circumstances, but Kwanh was no ordinary man. He'd spent ten years involved in jungle warfare, so it had to be more than that.

Bolan fell in beside Kwanh as they started back to the main road. He wanted to give the Vietnamese a chance to open the discussion, but Kwanh just ground his teeth. He continued to glance over his shoulder. Finally the Executioner took the bull by the horns. "Anything wrong?"

Kwanh shot him a look that suggested he might be looking at the village idiot, but remained silent. He just shook his head and closed the gap between him and the man in front.

Bolan caught up. "You seem like you're expecting someone."

Kwanh snorted. "Here? Who could I be expecting out here? No man in his right mind would expect anyone here."

"You don't seem surprised by any of this. It's almost like you knew it was going to happen."

"How could I have anticipated any of this?"

"You know the answer to that as well as I do."

"Then why don't you tell me? You seem to have made up your mind already. You might as well tell me what it is I'm supposed to know. That way I'll know it, and you'll be right."

"I think you know, or at least that you have some idea what happened back there. I think maybe you know who did it and why."

"I think you're a crazy man. That's what I think."

"You know better than that."

"Do I?"

Bolan didn't answer. He didn't have to. The truth was written all over Kwanh's face. Instead, he posed another question. "It's not over, is it?"

"What's not over?"

Before he could answer a sharp clap of thunder rattled the leaves. The sound broke in a wave and was followed by two more, no less thunderous. Grenades.

Salang's men panicked. They turned and started to run back toward Bolan. The lieutenant shouted to them to halt, but they were too frightened to listen. The lead man darted to the left, trying to dodge past Bolan, but the big man was too quick for him. He snaked out an arm and clotheslined the running soldier, who went down in a heap, gagging and clutching at his throat.

The man behind him, taking advantage of the distraction, darted to the right, but Kwanh leaped in front of him and blocked his path with his rifle. The Vietnamese shook his head, then said something in

Thai. The soldier cursed at him, then spit, narrowly missing Kwanh's feet. But he stayed where he was.

"What did you say to him?" Bolan asked while hauling the fallen soldier to his feet and holding him up with one hand.

"I told him his mother slept with Cambodians." Kwanh laughed, but it was a mirthless sound. "Race is a matter of pride out here, and the Cambodians are in the middle. They don't like the Thais and they don't like my people. The feelings are mutual."

Gunfire erupted on the road, followed by another thumping explosion.

Salang managed to halt the others by shouting a series of commands. The tone was unmistakable, even if the words were unintelligible to Bolan. And when the lieutenant stalked past his men to grab Bolan's prisoner by the shirt and swing him around, there was no way to misunderstand him. The man was furious. He started to harangue the men, who looked at their feet, and scratched the damp mulch with their boots. They were embarrassed at being frightened, and it seemed apparent that they were more afraid of Salang's threats than they were of anything waiting for them up ahead.

Bolan brushed past Salang and tugged Kwanh along in his wake. He turned to shout over his shoulder. "The jeeps..." Salang nodded, and the Executioner vanished into the jungle, Kwanh on his heels.

A furious firefight was getting under way, and there could be no doubt the jeeps and their guardians were under attack. As he dashed through the tangled undergrowth, Bolan couldn't help but wonder if this was what Kwanh had been waiting for. Or had he just guessed?

Either way it meant the Vietnamese had some explaining to do. But first they had to save the jeeps. It would be a long haul to the Khmer Rouge camp on foot, and the way Salang's men were acting, desertion was almost a foregone conclusion.

The exertion was taking its toll. Bolan was breathing heavily, and there was still two hundred yards to go. The gunfire was fast and furious, and it sounded as if the guards were putting up a good fight. That could only mean they were fighting for their lives.

Bolan neared the road, entered a strip of sparse undergrowth and slowed. Kwanh was right behind him. They waited for Salang and his men to catch up. Bolan told the lieutenant to string his men out along a hundred-yard line. Then, realizing the danger of a crossfire, he changed his mind.

Peeking through the growth, he could see nearly two dozen men firing alternatively. Three of the jeeps were smoking wrecks. A fourth was intact, but it had been tipped over on its left side.

The Thais had taken cover in the forest on the far side of the road. They were returning fire, but only sporadically. The attackers were sandwiched, but neither Thai contingent could shoot without running the risk of accidentally hitting its allies on the other side.

For the moment the beleaguered Thais didn't even know help had arrived.

Bolan waved Salang over. "Take half your men and get out on the right wing. I'll take the other half to the left."

Salang nodded. "Signal when you're ready to open fire."

"Right."

The lieutenant and his men lay flat on their stomachs and squirmed along behind the attacking line. The enemy forces were in uniforms, but Bolan didn't recognize them.

He whispered to Kwanh, "Know who they are?"

The Vietnamese nodded. "Chinese."

"Are you sure?"

"I'm sure."

Salang was in position. Bolan had his men ready and could just make out the Thai lieutenant almost two hundred yards away. He raised his hand, but before he could bring it down the Chinese charged across the road, firing indiscriminately, and took cover behind the jeeps. Return fire slammed into the wreckage, and bullets sailed into the forest, ripping at the leaves and snapping off smaller branches.

Bolan brought his hand down, then opened fire.

The Chinese were momentarily confused. Three men fell in the first few seconds before they realized they were being attacked from the rear.

They started to run back across the road, but the heavy fire was merciless. Two more men were cut down, and the others broke for the road. As they rushed past Salang's position, his men opened fire, picking off the lead runners. Those behind stopped in their tracks.

The Thais across the road rallied. They increased the pressure, breaking cover and charging into the open. Salang's men did the same. Bolan led his section out into the road and opened up as the Chinese attempted to fall back toward the jeeps.

The enemy was hopelessly trapped.

As the Thais fanned out into the road from both sides, the bulk of the Chinese sprinted up the rutted road. The Thai soldiers stood in the road, firing slowly, taking their time and aiming. They weren't having much luck as the Chinese veered into the trees. Salang sprinted to Bolan's side, puffing and holding his side. He gulped for air before asking, "Do you think we should go after them?"

Bolan glanced at Kwanh, who shook his head slightly. "Kwanh doesn't think so." Then, turning to the Vietnamese, he asked, "Why not?"

"There'll be more of them."

"But they're ahead of us. We can't stay here forever," Salang argued.

"They won't stay," Kwanh said.

Bolan was more convinced than ever that something was going on in Kwanh's head, some secret wheels were turning. He had to find a way to shake him up, to force him to tell what he knew. But before he could say anything Salang exploded.

"Damn it, I've already lost three men. Three of the jeeps are ruined and the fourth may or may not work. What are we supposed to do—let them disappear and walk home licking our wounds?"

"Walk home, no. Lick your wounds and let them disappear, yes. Believe me, we can't take them on." He waved one small, almost delicate brown hand toward the knot of Thai soldiers. "Look at them," he said, hardly trying to conceal his contempt. "Handpicked, you told us, and look what happened. Do you have any idea how long the Chinese have been in this part of Cambodia? Years. Some of these men have been here for fifteen years. They know this country like they know the veins on their wives' bellies. And there may be hundreds of them. The best thing we can do, Lieutenant Salang, and you better believe this, is to fall back and wait to see what happens."

"Fall back? To where? Where are we supposed to hide? And what good would it do? If they know the area as well as you say, they'll find us, anyway."

"But they don't want to find you. They aren't looking for Thais."

Bolan saw his opening and jumped through before it could close. "Who *are* they looking for, Kwanh?"

The man looked away, and Bolan could see the smaller man's back grow taut. Veins stood out in Kwanh's jaw, but Bolan wouldn't let go. "Tell me what's going on. Who are they looking for?"

The Viet turned back to him, licking his lower lip. "You already know, don't you?"

"Vietnamese troops. Is that it? Do you have men in the area?"

"I don't, no. But there may be Vietnamese troops, yes."

"May be? Are there or aren't there?"

Kwanh nodded. "Yes, there are."

"That's who ambushed the Khmer Rouge, isn't it?"

"Probably."

"So we walked into the middle of something you knew about, and three of Salang's men got killed. It could have been avoided, but you kept your mouth shut."

"Would it have made any difference? Would you have waited a day, two days, three, before charging in here, a place where you don't belong, to find a woman who doesn't belong here, either?"

"And I suppose you do belong here. Is that it?"

Kwanh shook his head sadly. "I don't belong, either. You're right about that. But if you had seen—"

"Don't feed me any of that self-righteous crap about how the Vietnamese saved the Cambodian people. I don't want to hear it."

Kwanh nodded. "All the same, it's true. But that's no longer important. We have to decide what we do now."

"Not until you tell me what other secrets you're keeping."

"None. Absolutely none. I didn't tell you before because there's no connection. It's just one of those unfortunate coincidences."

"I don't believe in coincidence, Kwanh."

5

Katherine May stepped into the room with a sense of dread. The soldier stood behind her, his hand resting on the doorjamb. This would be her third interrogation. The first two had been rough but not physical. She wasn't sure why, but kept her fingers crossed that this time would be no different.

She thought she'd prepared herself for anything, but she was wrong. Her interrogator wasn't present. In his place a small man with white hair sat behind a desk. He looked vaguely familiar, but she couldn't place him.

He watched her for more than a minute, his eyes flat and expressionless. She thought he might not even have blinked, but she wasn't sure. There was something mechanical about him, as if he ran on batteries. He moved one hand, and the entire arm seemed to shift awkwardly to accommodate the slight motion. Like a robot, she thought.

The door closed behind her. She was startled when it hit home, then swallowed hard and coughed to cover her nervousness.

The little man, whose face remained placid, suddenly seemed more animated. His cheekbones were high, his skin lighter in tone than she was used to. More Mongolian or Korean maybe. Or Chinese.

"Who are you?" he asked.

She was surprised at the softness of his voice. It sounded more than civil, almost kind. His Khmer was almost perfect, but not quite. There was the faint hint of something alien, an accent she couldn't put her finger on. Katherine hesitated. She didn't want to lie, couldn't afford it really. She didn't know how much they knew. But telling the truth in these circumstances was out of the question, at least telling the whole truth.

Her two previous sessions had been short, and she'd confined herself to terse answers, yes or no when she could manage it, a couple of words when she had to. She'd been truthful but not forthcoming. She had the distinct impression that today wasn't going to be as easy.

"Katherine," she said, her voice barely audible.

"Speak up," he ordered. "I'm getting to be an old man. I don't hear as well as I used to."

"Katherine," she repeated. "Katherine May."

"You are either a very courageous young woman or a very foolish one." He leaned forward, put his elbows on the desk and cupped his chin in both hands.

"I don't know what you mean."

The old man smiled, his face almost radiant. "Somehow I doubt that."

"Why are you asking me these questions?" she asked. "Why am I here?"

"You're here because you interfered in an affair that didn't concern you. At least I know of no reason why it *should* concern you. But perhaps I'm wrong. I'm asking you these questions because that's my job, and also because those who are concerned with the affair are, quite understandably, curious about the motives for your intrusion. Why were you at the Chulingorn camp?"

"I already told Comrade Serap the reason. That is *my* job."

The old man smiled. It was a pleasant smile and seemed almost genuine. Perhaps it was, she thought. But she knew it might just be a technique, and that it didn't really change her situation. "Oh, really? And what exactly is your job?" She started to answer, but he held up a hand. "I forget my manners. Would you care for something? Tea, perhaps?'

She nodded. The kindness was probably calculated, but as long as she realized it, she would be reasonably safe from entrapment. And sipping the tea would give her the opportunity to exercise a little control over the interview. "Yes, thank you."

The white-haired man tapped an old brass teacher's bell on his desk and leaned back in his chair. "No point in wasting electricity," he said, nodding at the bell. The door opened, and a woman entered. She was old, perhaps even older than the man behind the desk, but unlike him, she didn't wear her years comfortably. She was bent at the waist, and her mouth held few teeth, if any. Her voice shook when she asked what was desired of her, and her hands trembled. Possibly Parkinson's, Katherine thought, the professional in her clicking on as if by remote control.

When the old woman had gone, Katherine asked, "Who are you?"

"My name is Someth Phouma."

"Is it Comrade Phouma?"

The old man smiled slightly. "If I recall our earlier exchange, it was my job to ask questions, while yours had something to do with being at the camp. Why don't we just proceed on that basis?"

"As you wish."

"Good. Now, then, tell me why you were at the camp."

"I work for the World Refugee Council. Perhaps you've heard of it?"

"I have, yes. The West is full of such organizations. It's a wonder all the angels of mercy don't break each other's wings. Or do they?"

She shook her head. "There's much more misery in the world than you can imagine, Mr. Phouma. Very much more."

"And you think you can alleviate some of this misery. Is that it?"

"I try."

He nodded. "Is that all you do?"

"Yes."

"Then why did you make such an aggressive spectacle of yourself at Chulingorn? That isn't exactly the province of social workers and missionaries."

"And why not? There's as much poverty and disease at Chulingorn as there is anywhere else. Those people have virtually nothing to their names, nothing except their misery. But they had made their choice, and you have no right to deny it to them."

The door opened again, and the old woman entered. She carried a tray with a battered teapot and a pair of chipped cups. The hint of wretched elegance was incongruous in the room, and Phouma seemed aware of it. He waited until the old woman left, then picked up the teapot and one of the cups. "French," he said. "Colonial influence, fast receding into memory." He poured the tea for both of them, and Katherine stepped forward to take the cup he pushed toward her.

The tea was hot and bitter. As if he sensed her reaction to the taste, he said, "No sugar, unfortunately. You must like sugar, being so Westernized."

She shook her head, backed up two steps and sank onto the edge of a chair.

Phouma took a sip of his own tea, set the cup down and waited. After Katherine had taken another sip, he said, "Now, please, tell me exactly what you were doing at the refugee camp."

"I already told you. I was there for the council to monitor conditions in the camp. I was supposed to file a detailed report, focusing on the specific needs of the people. My agency would then attempt to fill those needs."

"Humanitarian relief. Is that what you're telling me?"

Katherine nodded.

"Does the name Trang Van Leung mean anything to you?"

So, here it comes, she thought. The iron hammer under the velvet veneer. She shook her head, then wondered whether it had been too vigorous a denial. It was touchy, this lying business. She knew that. She'd been coached, although in none of her training had there been the assumption that she'd be captured. She wasn't, after all, supposed to get this close to the enemy. That was Trang's job. "No, I don't think so," she replied. Her voice sounded deceitful even to her own ears. It was tight, brittle, pitched higher than normal. She felt her pulse racing just a bit, and the skin of her face and neck grew warm. She felt dampness trickle between her breasts and knew it had nothing to do with the weather. The temperature in the room hadn't changed in the past ten minutes, and suddenly she was leaking like a sieve.

"Odd," Phouma commented, running a hand through his white hair.

"Why odd?"

"Because you were the last one to see him alive."

She almost lost it altogether at that. She wanted to ask about him but couldn't decide how. If she did, Phouma might take it as a sign that she knew Trang.

But if she didn't ask, he might wonder why she had no natural curiosity about a man who supposedly had just died.

What should she do? She couldn't decide. Better, she thought, to err on the human side. "This Trang, he died recently?"

Phouma shook his head once quickly, seemingly surprised by her response. Maybe she could pull it off, after all.

"I don't think I know anyone by that name. Vietnamese, isn't it?" She was tempted to say more, but that would be pushing it. Better to let him make the next move.

"Perhaps you knew him by another name."

"Did he have another name? Maybe if you told me what it was, I could . . ."

"Could what, Miss May?"

"Could say whether I knew him."

Phouma sipped his tea. She was conscious then of the deadweight of the cup in her hand, and took another mouthful of the bitter fluid.

"I don't know whether he had another name or not," Phouma said finally.

Katherine wanted to change the subject. She knew he was leading her, because she hadn't seen Trang at Chulingorn. But that meant he knew she was *supposed* to see him. She was getting frightened now. Maybe if she asked him a direct question, he might follow her lead. If she was careful, she could skirt the mine field, instead of walking through it. She had a sudden flash of the gun in the hut. Was it still there?

"You're Khmer Rouge?" she asked.

"Of course."

"Are you Cambodian? You don't look it. More like a Cham maybe."

He smiled. "If I weren't Cambodian, would I be Khmer Rouge? My name is Laotian, but you're woman enough of the world to know that means nothing. After all, we have such a brutal reputation. No outsider would stand a chance, would he?"

"I'm sure I don't know. But it's little less than brutal to rip those people out of the camp like that and force them to come back."

"It's their homeland."

"They chose to leave it."

"They shouldn't have."

"That isn't your decision, Mr. Phouma."

"It has to be someone's. Why not mine?"

She had an answer for that, but knew she'd better not give it. Instead, she reminded him that she was no ordinary refugee. "My agency will be wondering where I am."

"For a while perhaps."

"They're very concerned about their workers' safety. Perhaps you could contact them and tell them I'm all right."

"I'm afraid not."

"Then perhaps you could take me back to Thailand?"

Phouma shook his head. "No, that's not in the cards, Miss May."

"But why? I don't understand—"

"You will. You see, I must know what you wanted with Trang."

"I already said I didn't know anyone by that name."

Phouma opened a drawer in the center of his desk, reached in and pulled out a wrinkled brown envelope. "Then perhaps you can explain this," he said, pushing the envelope across the desk.

She looked at the envelope but made no attempt to pick it up.

"Go on," he prodded. "Open it."

She bent down far enough to place the teacup on the floor, then leaned forward to take the envelope, which felt greasy. She put it in her lap but made no attempt to open it.

"You seem reluctant," Phouma observed. "Why don't you look? If you truly don't know Trang, then nothing in that envelope will cause you the least discomfort. On the other hand, if you do, or rather did, know him, that might very well be a different matter."

Katherine unfolded the flap and opened the envelope. She had no idea what the envelope might contain, but she steeled herself for the worst. Pulling out the sheet of paper inside, she realized the worst was far worse than she could have imagined. It was an old picture, three, maybe four years, but there was no mistaking her. Or Trang Van Leung.

She chewed at her lower lip thoughtfully.

"I'm afraid I have to ask you the same question, yet again, and for the last time," Phouma said. "What did Trang tell you?"

She looked at the photograph and shook her head. "I haven't seen him in years."

"You didn't see him at Chulingorn?"

She shook her head. "No."

"But you were supposed to?"

She nodded.

"Interesting," he said. "I would have sworn..." He let his voice die out and left her hanging.

It took a half hour to right the upended jeep and scavenge undamaged supplies from the three others that had been destroyed. Salang had posted two three-man teams to watch, one on either end of the column, nearly two hundred yards from the wreckage. Some of the packs were salvageable, and the contents of some of the others were still usable, despite the charring of the canvas. Much of the ammunition was intact, but many of the food containers had been split, and the food would be useless in a day or so. They were able to save some grenades and an RPG launcher, some first-aid supplies, and little else.

When they had salvaged as much as they could, they loaded the remaining jeep, leaving just enough room in the front for a driver. The three wounded would have to walk, one of them on makeshift crutches hacked from a bamboolike plant growing in abundance on both sides of the road.

Bolan had worried about the wounded. The injuries weren't serious, but the men would be a liability if they were attacked again. And there was no doubt in his mind they would be. He didn't know where or when, but he knew it was coming. The presence of the Chinese was ominous. Having Khmer Rouge to contend with was bad enough, but having foreign troops, probably much better trained and certainly better equipped, posed a significant threat.

Kwanh kept to himself now, probably embarrassed at having kept the presence of the Vietnamese unit a secret. It was no secret now, of course, possibly not even to the Chinese. And that could only make matters worse. The Chinese were almost certain to increase their patrols, possibly even to mount a full-scale search-and-destroy. A handful of Thais was little more than a nuisance, an annoying fly to be swatted.

The Thais, and Bolan along with them, could get caught in the middle and ground to a smear of blood and protoplasm, a feast for the jungle bugs, in the blink of an eye. But there was nothing to be done about it. Bolan had argued that the jeep ought to be sent back to Thailand with the wounded, but Salang had been adamant. He wouldn't send three men, protected only by one, and he couldn't spare more than one.

Better, he said, to wait, call for a helicopter and have the men airlifted out. But they had to move, to get away from the area because it was where the Chinese would start their search. They had to put as much distance as possible between themselves and the scene of the ambush.

But they had to move slowly so that the wounded could keep up. The jungle was strangely silent, and

Bolan had the eerie sensation that they were being watched. An advance patrol stayed out in front, three hundred yards ahead. The three men were cautious, watching for mines in particular, because the mine detector had been destroyed.

The sun was extremely hot, and the men kept to the side of the road, trying to use the shade for protection from its oppressive heat. But the higher the sun climbed, the less shade there was. After an hour it was straight overhead, filling the road with invisible fire. The only advantage lay in the fact that the sun was behind them. At least they could see, even if they couldn't avoid the hammering heat.

The man on crutches was losing his strength rapidly. The unit had covered almost two miles, and he was already falling behind. Two soldiers tried to help him, but his legs just wouldn't move properly. He was out on his feet.

Salang stopped the jeep and waited. With agonizing slowness the two soldiers carried their wounded comrade, letting the crutches fall onto the bone-dry road. At the jeep they hoisted him up and tied him on as if he were a piece of luggage. The man closed his eyes immediately and lay with one arm draped across his face to protect his eyes from the intense sunlight.

By three o'clock Bolan was counting the hours until sundown. This wasn't going to work. There was no doubt about it, and he thought maybe Salang would listen to reason now. He double-timed it to the head of the main column and fell in beside the lieutenant.

"We can't keep up like this," Bolan said. "We have to do something."

"I know that," Salang snapped. "But we have to go another three miles. The road is too narrow for a helicopter to land here. We can't take the time to carve a landing zone, and explosives would give us away. If we reach the river, there's room. Our maps aren't perfect, but I know we can find someplace for the helicopter to put down. You'll just have to be patient."

"Patience is one thing, but this just might be suicide."

"What do you mean?"

"You notice how quiet it is?"

"So?"

"So I have the distinct impression that they already know where we are. They're just waiting."

"Waiting for what?"

Bolan shook his head. "I don't know yet."

Kwanh watched the exchange, and Bolan glanced at him, thinking the Vietnamese might volunteer an opinion, but the small man kept his own counsel. They pushed on because there was nothing else to do. The humidity was getting more and more oppressive, and the sun started to wane a bit as a high haze drifted across the sky.

It would rain before long, and the road would turn into a quagmire. The men could manage, but the jeep would bog down. It was already groaning under the heavy weight. Salang, to his credit, seemed to realize it and told the driver to pick it up. The man at the wheel was already skittish, but he nodded. If there were mines in the road, maybe he'd be lucky.

Salang waved him on, telling him to keep the rest of the unit in sight, and sent the two wounded men along, one standing on either running board. The added weight caused the engine to groan as if it were being tortured, but it had to be done.

The rest of them broke into a double-time trot behind the jeep. The vehicle slowly pulled away as the clouds began to thicken. There was a little more than two miles to go, and by the look of the sky, they had fifteen minutes, at most, before the rains came.

The road broke to the right, and the jeep slowed a little, but still managed to drift out of sight. Bolan pumped it up another notch. Kwanh matched him stride for stride as they tried to catch up. Rounding the turn, the warrior noticed that the trees thinned a little, maybe a sign they were getting closer to the river.

The rest of the Thais were strung out behind Bolan in a ragged line. Glancing back, he saw them dragging their tails, barely able to put one foot in front of the other. Between the heat, humidity and the added weight of overloaded packs, they were quickly wearing down.

They'd need several hours to recuperate once they reached the river. But at least they'd have the wounded on a chopper, and the jeep would be theirs. With even a faint smile from fortune they might get another jeep on the inbound chopper and split the freight to something approaching a reasonable load.

The river finally came into view, a dank, swirling greenish-brown ribbon half a mile away. The jeep was almost there. The ruins of a bridge, splintered piles jutting up like the stubs of teeth from a broken jaw, marked the river crossing. A crossing might be possible if they got there before the rain started.

The first spatters of rain kicked up little puffs of dust on the road. The jeep was at the river now, and the Thai soldiers were tapping their energy reserves to cover the last few hundred yards. Their footsteps pounded on the road behind Bolan as the Executioner hit the flat bottom that stretched to the bank. On this side of the river the trees ran right down to the waterline. The jeep was already in the water, its running boards still above the waterline, but just barely.

On the far side of the river a wide grass-covered bank took up more than half an acre. It wasn't much, and it had a shallow pitch, but the chopper should be able to land. The jeep was struggling, its engine racing near flat out, but it was still moving.

Bolan waded in just as the jeep started to have trouble, followed by Kwanh, then Salang. The three men plunged toward the vehicle as it started to roll back, its engine roaring, its traction all but gone. They threw their shoulders into it. The jeep stopped its roll as the driver backed off a little on the engine, afraid he might throw a rod.

The footing was soft under the water. Bolan's feet sank into the mud, but he strained against the jeep. As Kwanh and Salang bent their backs into it, the jeep started forward again, Salang losing his footing and tumbling into the brown water.

The engine raced again as the wheels spun, then caught, and the jeep lurched ahead. They were climbing the other bank now. It wasn't too steep, but it was enough to make the overloaded jeep a handful. It rolled slowly but steadily, struggling up and out of the deepest water. Bolan could hear the faint dribble of draining water as the running boards came up over the surface again. The footing got better, and the jeep suddenly leaped ahead and up the bank.

Salang, soaking wet, snatched at the radio mike and raised the air base at Udorn. He requested a chopper, and he demanded it now. He argued for a couple of minutes, then slammed the mike down in disgust. Looking at Bolan, he said, "Two hours."

The Executioner nodded. It wasn't great, but it was better than nothing.

"And no second jeep," Salang added, then cursed in Thai. The veins on his neck and jawbone stood out like cables as he stomped up to the tree line. As his men straggled across the river, he shouted at them to hurry, then plopped down with his back against the thick trunk of a fallen tree.

There was no place to hide the jeep, but the men shrank back into the trees to wait for the helicopter. Bolan was uneasy about the delay. They were sitting ducks, and if he was right about having been spotted, it gave the Khmer Rouge or the Chinese—or both—plenty of time to plan a careful assault.

But he wasn't in charge of the Thais, and he wasn't about to go on alone. It would be near nightfall before the helicopter arrived, and with the thick clouds rolling by overhead, it was already getting dark. The rain had settled into a steady drizzle, the worst of its fury spent in the first few minutes.

With the incessant drumming of the water on the foliage, it was impossible to hear anything out of the ordinary. Salang had posted a couple of sentries, but both men were more interested in staying dry than in watching the perimeter.

There would be no radio contact until the chopper was right overhead, in order to maintain the last shreds of security they could wrap around themselves. After two hours of tense waiting, Bolan found himself pacing along the tree line.

He heard the chopper first, off in the distance, the sound of its rotors rising and falling as the wind shifted. Salang's radio crackled, and he rousted his men from the jungle's edge. The three wounded were herded down to the edge of the water. A finger of light speared out, then vanished.

Salang barked into the radio and the chopper veered closer. Again the light speared out, and this time the pilot could see them. The big Chinook, a U.S. Army veteran, wobbled in the air, then slowly drifted toward them.

The Thais gathered into a tight knot, and Bolan got to his feet, shouting as the Chinook started to settle.

Outlined in the searchlight, they were too easy a target. But the chopper drowned out his voice.

He started to run down the hill toward the men, circling to avoid the descending aircraft. The Chinook touched down, and the men surged forward, carrying their wounded comrades. At the open door of the chopper they started to hand the wounded up to a small detachment of medics and infantrymen.

Bolan heard Kwanh call out, but the words were swept away on the prop wash. He turned halfway around, then caught a sudden flash in the corner of his eye. He knew it was bad even before he'd swung his gaze back to the aircraft, which went up with a tremendous roar. A second flash lanced out from across the river.

This time he knew what it was.

The rocket slammed into the already mushrooming wreckage. The Chinook's fuel ballooned into a huge ball, and the concussion of the blast slammed into Bolan's chest like a huge fist, punching him flat on his back. The second blast scattered the flaming wreckage.

He could hear men shouting, and one man danced away like a demon, whirling around, flaming bits of cloth arcing away from his fuel-drenched body. For a moment Bolan thought it might be Salang, but there was no way to tell.

At almost the same instant two flares popped high overhead, then began their gentle descent, swaying slightly in the updraft from the burning Chinook. In the harsh glare Bolan could see men swarming down the road from the far side and into the river.

Someone grabbed him by the arm, and he looked up to see Kwanh clawing at him, trying to haul him to his feet. Bolan scrambled away, but Kwanh dragged him down, shouting, "Come on. It's too late for them."

"Salang..."

"Salang's dead! Come on!"

Bolan knew Kwanh was right. He stopped in his tracks as the first burst of gunfire ripped at the wreckage, scattering sparks and ricocheting off into the darkness.

The warrior raced to the jeep and grabbed an extra clip of ammunition for his M-16. As he was turning away, another rocket sailed across the river. It went high and detonated among the trees. Bolan sprinted for cover, but a heavy tree smashed into his leg. His ankle twisted by the blow, he fell to his knees. A wave of pain seared his leg as he tried to get up. Kwanh tugged at his sleeve, dragging him into the jungle.

KATHERINE SAT IN THE HUT, listening to the noises of the night. She hadn't bargained on this, but she'd be willing to bet that Bishop had. The bastard was always holding out on her. The real question was what was he doing about it. She didn't have to think about it much to know the answer.

Nothing.

She was angry, and she blamed herself, but she blamed him, too. The ball was in her court. If anything was going to get her out of this mess, it would have to be something she did for herself.

Phouma was playing games with her. He'd known all along that she knew Trang. He'd teased her, let her walk the tightrope, waiting for her to fall. She hadn't, but she'd come close. She'd lost her balance, teetered and moved on.

And the bastard had waited until she was almost across the chasm before he gave her a push. Those photographs proved very little, but they were enough. She knew that immediately. And Phouma knew that she knew. She could still see the smile on his face as she'd looked up.

But she was puzzled. He hadn't pressed his advantage. After she'd seen the photographs, he'd taken them back and put them into his desk. He'd said nothing, nor did he appear to be angry. His face had turned hard but not cruel. He was playing another game, with different rules, rules she could only guess at. Instead of being a player in Phouma's game, she was just a piece, something to be moved around the board.

But like any game, there were limits. And the one that mattered was time. If Phouma thought he could wait her out, he'd be willing to go easy on her. But once he decided she wasn't going to crack, he'd turn up the heat. She'd seen enough of that before she'd made it to Thailand, and it was enough to last her a lifetime.

At the end of that road there was nothing but a bullet in the back of the head. She'd be one more nameless corpse rotting in a hole. It seemed terrifying to contemplate, but what was one more when the toll was already two million? Who would even notice one more skull turned up by a plow twenty years from now?

She had to do something, but what? One woman, alone, with a gun and eighteen bullets. How could she possibly make it back? She wasn't even sure where she was. But the Khmer Rouge would certainly find her long before she got close to the border. It was impossible.

But she had to try.

The decision calmed her nerves. She walked to the door of the hut and listened. She could hear something, probably mice, scurrying among the palm leaves of the thatching. There was a guard, she knew, but that couldn't be helped. She felt over the lintel for the gun. After a minute of groping, she still hadn't found it, and she started to panic.

Standing on tiptoe, she dug her hand deeper into the thatch. Her fingertips brushed something cold, and she thought she'd found it, but whatever it was moved. She recoiled, thinking it must be a snake. A second later the thing, whatever it was, crawled out of the thatch. She couldn't see it clearly, but knew it wasn't a snake after all. Probably a lizard.

She tried again to find the gun. This time she got lucky. It had slid down into the leaves a little, and it was perilously close to falling through to the outside. Using her fingers like a pair of tweezers, she managed to squeeze the checkered grip tightly enough to pull the gun up an inch or so.

The rest was easy. The spare clip, not as heavy as the gun, was right where she'd left it. With the weight of the pistol in her hand, she'd expected to feel more confident. But the Browning had the opposite effect. With the deadweight of the automatic in her hand, she couldn't pretend any longer that this was just an exercise. It was real, as real as the cold metal in her hand. And if she had to use the gun, she'd be taking a human life.

It was that thought that frightened her most of all. She was supposed to be saving lives, not threatening them. But her idealism was on the naive side, something a friend back in the States had told her over and over again. The bad guys don't give a damn about humanitarianism, Lori had told her. That was why they were called bad guys. It wasn't enough to be prepared to die in order to save the world. That was the easy part. To succeed, a person had to be ready to kill. Katherine didn't think she'd understood it until now. Now, when it was probably already too late.

She tucked the spare clip into her pocket and stepped back to the door. She could hear a buzzing sound, like a large insect hovering off to the left. It took her a moment to realize her guard was snoring. That was a break she hadn't counted on. All she had to do was to cash in on it. She backed away from the door, terrified of what she was about to do, but more terrified still of what might happen if she didn't try.

Katherine dropped to the ground when she felt the thatching against her back. She sat there in the darkest corner, oblivious of the dampness of the earth under her. Unlike most huts in this part of Cambodia, the camp wasn't built on stilts. It sat on the ground, the bare ground flooring each of the feeble structures she'd been in. There was something impermanent about it, and that frightened her.

She'd heard the stories of roving Khmer Rouge "security" teams. Moving from place to place, they visited an area with the suddenness of lightning, purging the villagers of suspected "counterrevolutionaries," then moving on. They were death squads, short and simple, vehicles of terror, and nothing else. The more simpleminded of the peasants—those who still survived—tried to use them to even personal scores. They'd turn in a neighbor who had something they wanted for themselves, or pay back a slight, real or imagined, by filing a complaint.

Within days, sometimes within hours, those accused of some sort of counterrevolutionary thinking would disappear. Sometimes there would be a small "work detail," the accused carrying rakes or hoes over their shoulders, sent off for a dose of reeducation. But those work details never came home. Usually there would be gunfire in the night and a mound of fresh earth in the morning.

No questions were asked. No one dared.

In the first days of the terror there had been open pits and gunfire night and day. But the incessant slaughter had been numbing, almost like anesthesia. This was far worse because it came so suddenly, without warning and without reason.

Katherine May feared that she was in the hands of such a security team. It seemed hard to believe. Phouma was so mild-mannered, so civilized. But the bureaucrats of death were no less prim and proper than any other breed of paper pushers. Phouma wouldn't pull the trigger, of course. That wasn't his job. But he, and people like him, seldom had a shortage of volunteers to handle the less tidy details.

She realized she was wrestling with some way to justify staying where she was, but there was no justification other than suicide. That was a fact as cold and as hard as the barrel of the Browning in her lap. To stay was to die. To flee might also be to die, but at least it would be on her own terms.

And she just might make it. There had to be people out there in the countryside who were fed up with the Khmer Rouge. It wasn't just the Vietnamese army that had driven Pol Pot to this tiny corner of Cambodia, or forced his minions up on their hind legs like trapped rats, their yellowed fangs bared in a final, desperate frenzy. It had been Cambodia itself, the land and its people. The farmers and the laborers—those in whose name the revolution had been waged—were the big losers, and they knew it.

Or did they?

They had to. That was all there was to it. And she had to find them.

Katherine got up almost reluctantly, conscious for the first time of the slime on her jeans. She wiped the seat of her pants, then scraped the filth onto the brittle thatch. She pulled the Browning out and snicked off the safety.

Tiptoeing to the door of the hut, she paused to listen. The buzz-saw snore still rose and fell. It was irregular but seemed genuine. The Browning was silenced, so she had that going for her. But it was about the only edge she did have.

She leaned out of the open door and looked at the guard. His chest rose and fell. The red band around his head fluttered a little as a breeze curled around the edge of the hut. The rest of the camp was dark and silent.

Katherine knew there would be guards posted, but neither how many nor where they'd be. The quickest way out was right past the main building, where Phouma had his office and, presumably, slept. There was almost certain to be a guard on it. Her legs wobbled as she stepped out of the hut. She felt lightheaded for a few seconds, drew in her breath sharply and waited for the trembling to subside.

When the tremor had passed, she eased around the corner of the hut, backing slowly, keeping close to the wall of the building. At the corner she waited for a moment, backed up another step to look along the edge of the building and, when she saw no one, sidestepped away from the guard.

Katherine dropped to a crouch and crept along the side wall of her hut. She could see the dim shadows of several other huts, a ragged half circle outlined against the dark mass of the forest behind them. Shaking her head as if answering a question, she sprinted into the open. Her feet sounded like thunder on the soft ground, but she knew it was just her imagination.

At the first of the huts she stopped to listen again. Nothing. A single fire, almost burned out, lay at the center of the camp, its coals glowing a dull red under a coating of ash. It threw no light at all beyond the shallow pit in which it had been built.

The jungle yawned darkly fifty yards away. It held its own terror, but it also offered a sort of safety. Taking a deep breath, Katherine sprinted for the black wall of trees. She was almost there when someone shouted. She wasn't sure whether it had anything to do with her, but she ran faster, her legs pumping.

The first branches whipped at her face and outstretched hands. She stumbled, regained her balance and slipped into the jungle.

Another shout shattered the stillness behind her, but it was too late to stop now.

Bolan was limping heavily. The tree limb had wrenched his ankle, and he could feel it swelling inside his boot, the bruised flesh pressing against the leather. It didn't bend easily, and every step sent a little spurt of flame up his leg.

Kwanh was leading the way, but he was exhausted, and his pace had begun to flag. Behind them they could hear the thrashing progress of their pursuers. Healthy, they could have put plenty of distance between them and the hounds on their trail, eventually gotten far enough ahead to lose them completely. But this was another matter. It was a straight run, and Bolan hoped Kwanh knew where he was going.

It was nearly dark. The rain had stopped and the sun spilled an orange wash through the undergrowth, but it wouldn't last long. Bolan wasn't sure whether that would be a blessing or a plague. They'd certainly be harder to spot in the night jungle, but they'd have to slow to a crawl. His damaged ankle would only get worse. It was possible that by morning he might not be able to put any weight on it at all. They kept moving because they had no choice.

Somewhere to the east he heard the throb of a heavy diesel. There had to be a road out there, no more than a couple of miles away, probably closer, given the way the jungle swallowed sound. And a diesel meant a truck. A truck meant reinforcements, possibly more beaters to begin thrashing the undergrowth to drive them like foxes before the hounds.

Kwanh slowed, doubled over and gasped for breath. He looked pale, and his skin was pasty. Beads of sweat covered his forehead and cheeks. They glistened in the orange light and made a brilliant orange smear on his upper lip. He had the dry heaves and clutched his stomach with both hands.

Bolan leaned in close. "Can you make it?"

Kwanh nodded, then heaved again. His stomach was empty, but the convulsion racked his body. He shivered uncontrollably. Wiping his face with his left sleeve, the Viet took a deep breath. He tried to talk, but his words were choked back by another convulsive spasm. He licked his lips, his mouth so dry that Bolan could hear the rasp of the man's tongue on his chapped lips.

"Not far now," Kwanh gasped. He dropped to a squat and bent way over, trying to get control of his stomach. He breathed deeply and slowly, holding each breath a long time, then letting it out in a series of short puffs. It seemed to be working, but there was so little time.

Bolan could hear the crashing in the jungle behind them much more clearly. Their pursuers were getting too close for comfort. He wished he knew what they were up against. The uniforms were those of the Khmer Rouge, but the men didn't look Cambodian. Kwanh thought they were Chinese, but Bolan wasn't sure.

The thought of the Chinese presence concerned the warrior. It was one thing to have a small unit of advisers; it was another to have a significant army, perhaps battalion strength, in the area. He wondered whether that might be the sort of information Katherine May was supposed to receive from Trang. Perhaps Trang had told her something significant. Salang was sure they hadn't had a chance to exchange a word, but there was no way to tell. And to answer that question definitively they'd have to find her. The prospect seemed more daunting by the second.

Kwanh straighted and leaned over to look past Bolan, back down the trail. He held a finger to his lips and motioned the warrior to the ground with both hands. Bolan dropped to his stomach and pivoted, rolling to the left to get off the trail.

"Look!" Kwanh whispered, and Bolan brushed aside a palm frond to stare back into the darkening jungle. On the trail, his head turned back in the direction he'd come, a solitary man took a step forward, then another. Bolan strained to hear whether the man was talking to anyone or simply so nervous that he was as concerned about what might be behind him as he was about what he knew was ahead of him.

In better circumstances the Executioner would have tried to take him alive, but the ankle killed that possibility. He drew the silenced Beretta and took aim. As far as Bolan could tell, there was no one directly behind him.

Kwanh joined him. "Can you hit him from here?" he whispered.

Bolan nodded. "If I get him, can you drag him off the trail without help?"

"I'll have to."

The Executioner waited for his target to finish a half turn, then squeezed the trigger gently. The man jerked sideways and fell to one knee. He started to turn his head, but Bolan fired a second shot that impacted high on the man's shoulder, just below the collarbone. Kwanh was already on his feet, moving back toward the wounded man. He picked up the guy's AK-47 and looped the strap of a canvas bag over his shoulder before heading toward Bolan at a dead run.

"Let's go," Kwanh panted, stopping just long enough to reach down and help Bolan to his feet. "We don't have much farther to go. You want me to help you?"

The warrior shook his head. "No thanks. Just stay out front. You can move more quickly than I can. You might as well be on the point. Besides, you know the terrain a hell of a lot better than I do."

"That's not been much help so far, has it?" Kwanh said.

"Maybe our luck'll change. Go on."

He watched the smaller man walk forward. When he was about fifteen or twenty feet ahead Bolan fell in behind him, trying to keep his weight off the ankle. The brief layover, rather than helping, had only made the injury worse. The muscles had begun to stiffen, and the ankle would hardly bend at all. The pain was still there, but there was a kind of numbness, too. He knew his body was manufacturing its own anesthetic to help kill the pain, but he also knew that the more he used it, and the less he rested, the more likely he was to create a long-term problem for himself. It couldn't be helped.

The diesel's rumble was still there, though more muted now. He didn't know whether that meant the truck was farther away, or that it had stopped moving and was simply idling. The two men were running parallel to the road, but Kwanh refused to change course. With Bolan's leg getting worse by the minute, he couldn't really argue.

Bolan's ankle gave out, and he fell heavily to the ground. He struggled up, resting his weight on one knee. The ankle wasn't going to get him much farther, and he knew it.

Kwanh had heard him fall and ran back to help. The Vietnamese was too small to be much help carrying the big American. He used a machete to hack at some bamboo, ignoring the racket the blade made slashing at the hollow stalks. He managed to get one—nearly two inches in diameter—and quickly cut it to size.

"Use this," he said. "It's not a crutch, but..." He shrugged.

Bolan took the smooth tube and tried putting his weight on it. It stayed rigid, and he managed to hobble a few paces without putting any strain on the bad ankle. The thrashing had resumed in the forest behind them.

"Hurry," Kwanh urged. He turned and sprinted down the trail. The lowering darkness swallowed him almost completely. Bolan glanced back and saw light. Several bright beams slashed at the underbrush, spearing through dense clumps of leaves and tossing swirling shadows. The sky overhead had turned dark gray.

The warrior had difficulty keeping up. The bamboo helped, but he was still limping badly. Kwanh bobbed in and out of view, a lighter shadow against the blackness. Limbs slashed at Bolan's face and hands. He lowered his head to protect his eyes and used his free hand to sweep some of the obstructions aside.

Suddenly he felt no obstacles. Expecting resistance, he lost his balance and fell to the ground. The bamboo rolled away.

Kwanh rushed to Bolan's side. "Forget the crutch," he whispered, hauling Bolan up and draping one arm around his shoulders.

Another obstacle loomed, and it took Bolan a moment to realize they were in an abandoned village. Kwanh mumbled something under his breath as he half pulled, half carried Bolan forward. He bypassed the first hut, then the second. At the third he stopped and looked around. The beams of light slashing at the jungle were dim but getting brighter.

"In here," Kwanh said, dragging the Executioner through the doorway.

He heard Kwanh scraping around in the dark, then a thud.

The Vietnamese took him by the arm. "Here. Be careful. One more step. All right." Kwanh let go and whispered, "Get down on your hands and knees. Hurry!"

Bolan complied, then heard a thump. A hand grabbed his wrist. "Careful, careful."

The warrior realized Kwanh was somehow standing below him and reaching up. "A bunker," he whispered.

"Never mind. Get down."

Bolan lay flat and spun around. He felt the ground fall away beneath his legs, just as a loud shout shattered the silence, followed by a crash of breaking branches, and another, more distant shout.

He slipped through a hole, and Kwanh guided him down, placing a hand on his shoulder. "Watch your head. Hurry, get down!"

The shouts were louder still, and Bolan could hear running feet. He stared at the hatchway above his head, unconsciously looking for a trace of light. He gripped the M-16 tightly, the safety off, the muzzle pointed straight up.

He heard someone in the hut overhead, but there was no sign of light. The man above either had none, or the hatch was a perfect fit.

Bolan crouched, trying to control his breathing, and in the back of his mind was a puzzling contradiction. Kwanh had probably just saved his life—but how did he know about this place?

The man seemed to be forthright, but he seemed to know things he shouldn't.

Someone else came into the hut, and Bolan tensed as the searchers exchanged a few words. He glanced toward Kwanh, wondering whether the Vietnamese understood the conversation above, but he couldn't see the little man in the darkness.

Shouts echoed through the village as several other men joined the search.

It was going to be a long night.

BOLAN OPENED HIS EYES, then focused on the illuminated dial of his watch—5:45 a.m. He listened carefully for a minute before moving. It was so quiet in the pit that he could hear water drip from the wall and plop softly on the damp ground.

He tried to flex his ankle, but the least motion sent a stabbing pain shooting up past his knee. He gritted his teeth against the agony and broke out in a cold sweat. He was cramped and sore in every muscle and joint.

"Kwanh?" he whispered.

No answer. He tried again, louder this time.

Again there was no response. He remembered the canvas pack and groped for it in the dark. His fingers finally found the rough cloth, and he latched onto the shoulder strap, hauled the pack close and felt for the small straps holding the flap closed. He tugged the small buckles open, flipped open the pack and felt inside—a small pistol, a box, probably of ammunition, and a clip loaded with what felt like 9 mm cartridges. Finally he felt the outlines of a small flashlight. He pulled the cylinder out of the pack and slid the switch forward. It clicked, and a beam of light stabbed across the small chamber, leaving a circle of light on the opposite wall.

He played the beam around the chamber. Kwanh was gone. He'd known it even before he'd found the light, but wanted evidence he couldn't deny. He examined the chamber while lying on one hip. The room was small, maybe ten feet each side. The ceiling above him seemed lower than it actually was. He could probably stand erect, but there would be little or no room to spare.

Three of the four walls were identical—blank faces of damp claylike soil, sweating beads of water that trickled down the wall and collected in small pools along the base of each wall, where trenches had been cut to keep the rest of the floor reasonably dry.

The fourth wall was a little different. A small square, blacked and framed with rough four-by-four timber, occupied its center right at floor level. It swallowed the beam easily, as if the opening ran on forever.

Bolan tried to get up, but his ankle hurt too much when he got to his knees. Standing was possible but pointless. He couldn't walk, not very far, anyway, and running was out of the question.

Never one to shrink from the impossible, he worked his way around the problem by hauling himself across the floor, sliding on his left hip and keeping his injured ankle rigid. When he reached the opening, he trained the beam inside. He couldn't see a back wall, but rows of damp four-by-fours marched off in regular ranks on either wall and across the ceiling.

The opening was a yard wide and less than a yard high. He was curious about where the tunnel might lead but reluctant to enter it. As far as he could see into its recesses, there was no place for him to turn around with anything short of gymnastic flexibility. Rapid movement wasn't even a consideration in so tight a space.

Whoever had designed the tunnel had in mind someone considerably smaller than Mack Bolan. He remembered the tunnels of Cu Chi in Vietnam and was less than anxious to see how close this tunnel was to those infamous catacombs. Those had been an impenetrable maze, and booby-trapped at every turn. Designed by the VC, their very dimensions were an impediment for the larger Americans.

But if there was a resemblance here, it might mean there were larger chambers somewhere ahead. If

Kwanh meant to betray him, which was more than a remote possibility, it just might save his life if he wasn't in the tunnels when the Vietnamese came back—if he even meant to return.

Ignoring the pain, Bolan crept back to the pack. He inventoried the contents, took what he thought he could use and shoved it into his own pack, then buckled it up. He found his M-16 and hooked both it and the pack with his left arm. Dragging himself back to the opening, he shoved the pack through and crawled in after it.

He felt a sense of urgency now, knowing that there was no place to hide until he found either a side tunnel or a chamber somewhere in the darkness ahead. Right now all someone had to do was point an assault rifle into the shaft and pull the trigger.

The ground was damp, and his clothes collected mud as he scraped ahead a foot at a time, shoving the pack and then hauling himself after it. It was difficult to gauge how far he'd traveled because he couldn't see behind him very well, even with the help of the flashlight. But in for a penny, he thought. After what must have been eighty or ninety feet, he was soaked in sweat, his front coated in a thick sheen of clay. Training the light ahead, he thought he saw something dark to the left. He tried to remember the orientation of the huts from the night before but wasn't sure which way he'd been facing when he entered the tunnel.

It made sense that each of the huts might have a chamber beneath it, and a shaft connecting to the others, perhaps in a central chamber. Then he realized a smart builder wouldn't have the central chamber anywhere near the huts. In the case of artillery bombardment, the huts would be natural targets. The point of a system of tunnels like this one was safety, and the farther away from the center of the village you were, the safer you would be.

Bolan crawled another ten feet, and the dark patch on the left grew more distinct. There was no doubt about it now—it was another shaft. He pushed the pack farther ahead, picking up his pace a little, but not enough to make a real difference. He could only use one leg to propel himself through the narrow opening, and the snail's pace was maddening.

At the intersection he stopped to listen, but could hear nothing but an occasional plop of falling water. He traveled ahead another foot and shined his light down the connecting tunnel. It seemed as endless as the one he'd just crawled through. That shaft continued on, curving slightly to the right. It could have been a difficult choice to make, but not knowing where he was made it a simple coin toss.

Negotiating the turn was no easy affair. He had to lie on his side and bend his upper body into the new tunnel, then haul his legs in after his trunk. Even so, he had to flex his legs to the maximum before he could pull them in. He managed to get far enough in that he could lie flat again, and took a breather.

After a couple of minutes, he summoned the energy to push on. His arms were screaming for relief, his shoulder sockets felt as if they had been set on fire, but he had to continue. He drew some satisfaction from the fact that he was no longer in sight of the original chamber. If they wanted to kill him, they'd have to find him first. And that thought brought him back to Kwanh.

Where had he gone, and why?

It was possible the Vietnamese had some connections in the area, maybe a network of contacts who kept him informed. Perhaps he'd gone to get help. But it was also possible the man had left him there to sink or swim on his own. Putting himself in Kwanh's shoes, he realized the temptation would be strong to do just that.

The man owed him nothing, and the warrior was a millstone around Kwanh's neck. Hobbled by the injury, he couldn't travel, and probably wouldn't be able to for two or three days at the earliest. Leaving Bolan behind might have been a painful but logical choice. The Vietnamese colonel had his own agenda, and Bolan didn't figure in it much. Why risk compromising himself and his priorities for a man he barely knew and almost certainly didn't like?

But Bolan had left the worst case until last. Kwanh might have gone to turn him in. Contacts worked two ways. Maybe the Executioner was no more than a poker chip, or a down payment on the IOU that might come in handy one day. That, too, was logical, and Kwanh was nothing if not logical.

There were no answers that made any difference, only guesses, and Bolan shoved them aside to concentrate on his current predicament. Fifty feet down the new shaft he found himself suddenly going downhill. The descent started slowly, then gradually escalated. Within fifteen feet he was headed down at a fifty-five-degree angle. The wet clay was so slippery that he could move with very little effort now, gliding like an otter a few feet at a time.

The slide bottomed out suddenly, and the warrior twisted his head and shined the light back up the incline. He'd descended a good twenty-five or thirty feet. Looking ahead, he saw a continuation of the shaft, once again flat and once again disappearing at the far end of the flashlight's beam. He spotted what might be another shaft nearly thirty feet ahead. As he moved on, he felt a steady trickle of water, looked up at the ceiling and found a narrow fissure through which the water, full of silt, dribbled at a steady rate. Groundwater no doubt, but it made him aware of how easily the tunnels might fill up. A heavy rain might flood them in a matter of minutes.

And that thought made him realize something else—there had to be allowance for that possibility. Either that or the builders weren't as smart as he thought they were. As if in response to his realization, the ground suddenly shook. A distant rumble echoed through the tunnel, and a few clods of damp clay fell on his outstretched arms. Was it thunder?

There was another tremble, and he could feel the ground shift under him, a shivering, as if he were prostrate on a bowl of gelatin. It wasn't until the third rumble that he realized it wasn't thunder. It was artillery, mortars probably.

Another one, this time much closer, and he felt a rush of air. One of the huts must have been hit. He felt helpless, as if the ground were about to close around him.

Another detonation shook the ground as the pack suddenly fell from beneath his extended hand. A second later he tumbled down off a lip of clay. He felt rough wood as he fell and landed heavily on his outstretched arms.

The impact knocked the wind out of him, and he realized he'd lost the light. It lay off to one side, its lens stuck in the mud, glowing palely, as if the earth were on fire beneath it.

He reached out and snared the light and wiped the lens clean on the sleeve of his shirt. Playing the light around him, he found himself in a large room. Its walls were timbered, and its roof was shored with thick beams, as if it had been excavated and a timber roof laid down before the dirt was pushed back.

The ground shook once more, and dirt sifted down from joints in the roof. Bolan closed his eyes and waited, not knowing whether his next breath would be his last.

The rumbling ceased, and the ground finally stopped shaking. The room in which Bolan found himself had several exits, every wall having at least one opening. He found the sack and his rifle. The fall did no permanent damage, but it hadn't helped his injured leg.

He dragged himself toward the nearest opening and trained the flashlight into the tunnel. Like the others he'd seen, this one seemed limitless. Before deciding, he wanted to check the others, as well, at least those he could reach without resorting to one of the wooden ladders that led to the higher openings, like the one he'd just fallen through.

One by one he examined the tunnels as far back as the light allowed. As he checked the last one, the beam flickered, and he cursed softly. Without the light he'd be almost helpless in the underground maze. He shook the flashlight, and the bulb flickered again, then grew brighter.

As he stepped forward, he heard a voice. It was distant, nearly swallowed by its own echo, but unmistakable. Someone had entered one of the tunnels. But which one?

Bolan waited for the sound to be repeated. After more than a minute, he heard it again. Someone was shouting. It crossed his mind that Kwanh might have returned and begun to look for him. The echo filled the chamber, but he couldn't tell which tunnel it came from. It didn't seem to be the one he'd fallen from.

Crawling to the wall, he hauled himself erect, putting weight only on his good leg and balancing himself with one hand on one of the wooden ladders. The voice shouted again.

It was impossible to recognize the speaker as Kwanh so garbled was the echo. Bolan tried to haul himself up the ladder, but his ankle was too tender to take his weight. He let go of the ladder and used the light to find his bag and rifle. As he tugged the bag toward him, a faint light glimmered from one of the tunnel mouths. The warrior extinguished his own light and stared at the hole in the wall.

There was no doubt about it. Someone was in the tunnel, and close enough that a flashlight beam, faint but still discernible, could reach the chamber. Again he heard a shout, and it came from the same tunnel.

Bolan shoved his bag into another tunnel and crawled in after it. He scrambled as quickly as he could, hoping to reach an intersection before anyone spotted him. Nearly a hundred feet in he found what he was looking for. The tunnel swerved slightly to the right, and he bent his body around the curve and out of sight. More important, he was out of the line of fire.

He continued on around the curve, putting a little more distance between himself and the chamber. He could risk using the light now, since he was heading away from the large room, and he clicked it on for a second. In its beam he found another opening, off to the right, about fifty feet ahead. Still leery of the weakening batteries, he clicked the light off and started shoving the bag ahead again. About thirty feet farther on a square of illumination appeared on the left-hand wall.

It was so unexpected that its significance didn't register immediately. Then it did—someone else was in the network. He had a man ahead and a man behind.

The block of light was pale, but the warrior still had twenty feet to go. By the time he reached his goal, he was certain to be seen. He could wait and shoot when the man turned in the tunnel, but rifle shots would be heard by the other man. And the disturbing thought that couldn't be ignored was that if there were two, there could be more.

Bolan slid the bag back along his body to get it out of the way, then crawled forward as fast as he could. The light was growing brighter and brighter. He could hear the approaching man grunting and gasping with the exertion.

Two feet from the opening he waited. The light was almost white now, the man's breathing so loud that he couldn't be more than five to ten feet away. Pulling the silenced Beretta, Bolan propped himself on his elbows and sighted on the mouth of the tunnel.

A distant voice drifted through the tunnel. A much louder voice, much closer to Bolan, answered. It was the man just five feet away. Bolan steeled himself and tensed for the shot. Now there were three, at least, in the maze with him. The light grew perceptibly brighter, then the flashlight itself was right in front of him.

Bolan squinted past the blinding light and could make out the mouth of the connecting tunnel through the red haze. The arm, with the flashlight extended, momentarily waved the light as the man pulled himself through. A split second later the man's head emerged.

The warrior squeezed off a round, and a 9 mm slug struck its target point-blank. The man's head dropped into the dirt, and the flashlight rolled against the far wall, its beam pointed back past Bolan's left shoulder.

He heard another shout from far down the connecting tunnel, cupped his hands over his mouth and shouted an unintelligible reply, hoping the sound was muffled enough to confuse his enemy. If it worked, he'd bought himself a couple of minutes.

Bolan grabbed the light, then reached back along his body for the canvas sack. He hooked it over his arm and started to crawl past the open mouth. He used the light for a few seconds, extinguished it and started to move as fast as he could. The bag kept rubbing against the left wall, but it was better than pushing it along in front of him. This tunnel seemed a little larger than the others had been. He still didn't have enough room to get on his hands and knees, but at least he could make better time.

Another shout echoed, this one from behind. He couldn't tell whether it was from the side shaft or from the chamber far behind him. He didn't bother to answer this time, but the shout spurred him on. His ankle remained stiff, and it was getting more painful as he used it to push himself along.

Fifty or sixty feet later he suddenly felt open space around him. He clicked on the light and found himself in a large chamber. Crates lined two walls, and the ashes of a recent fire filled one corner. The wall and ceiling above it were blackened with soot, and a small wooden trapdoor, unmarked by the fire, was mounted on the ceiling. The warrior assumed a smoke hole had to be behind it, then wondered whether it might be something larger than that. The trapdoor was certainly large enough. It was worth a look.

Bolan hauled himself up and reached for a pull cord attached to a peg. Balancing on his good foot, he extended himself full length, grabbed the cord and gave it a yank. The peg came free and the door swung down. As he suspected, there was a hole.

But it was too small.

More than one voice echoed in the tunnels now as more men joined the hunt, like ants on the trail of a lump of sugar. Three of the openings glowed faintly.

Bolan watched them for a second, debating whether to stand and fight or try to find a way out.

The voices faded a little as he pushed himself to leave the chamber. There was another bend, and he found himself in a section with a higher roof. He was able to crawl now. He picked up his pace as he rounded the long, sweeping curve. Ahead, a block of light marked the floor—and light from above meant a shaft to the surface.

When the light fell on the back of his neck, Bolan looked up. He was in a small room, no more than four feet on each side, and the sun was almost directly overhead.

There was a ladder, which he could almost reach. If he jumped, he might make it. Making sure the pack and rifle were secure, he balanced on his good leg, bent it at the knee and sprang up. His finger grazed the bottom of the lowest rung, but he couldn't get a grip. He landed heavily, instinctively cushioning his descent with both feet. The landing sent a wave of fire up his right leg, which buckled, then gave way. He staggered, trying to keep his balance, and backed into the wall.

But he stayed on his feet. Gathering his strength, he leaned back, gingerly holding the bad leg off the ground. When the pain subsided, he took a deep breath and hobbled back. He heard a loud shout down the tunnel he'd just left. The clamor seemed to galvanize him.

Again he coiled his one good leg and leaped. This time he caught the rung and hung on. With all his strength he hauled himself up until he could secure a grip on the next rung.

Bolan pulled his feet up as a burst of automatic gunfire slammed into the damp clay. A moment sooner and it would have taken his legs off at the knees. As it was, he was too busy to think about what might have happened. The pack scraped against the wall of the shaft as he climbed.

The surface seemed a mile away as he negotiated the widely spaced rungs with difficulty. The shaft had been designed for much smaller bodies. It was warm in the shaft, and he could feel the sweat dripping from his hair and running down his collar.

His leg hurt like hell, and he couldn't use it for anything more than a stopgap as he hauled himself up by brute force, letting his arms do most of the work. On alternate rungs he could lever himself with the good leg, but the rungs were spaced so far apart that even that put a strain on his injured ankle. Below and behind men were racing toward the shaft, and the Executioner knew he'd be a sitting duck unless he was up and out before they reached it.

Finally Bolan could reach the lip of the earth. He hauled himself up the last couple of feet and lay flat on the ground for a moment, breathing in the fresh, sweet air.

A voice carried up from below—one of his pursuers had reached the bottom of the shaft. Bolan risked a quick look over the edge, but a short burst nearly took his head off. He backed away, waiting for the man to start up the ladder. Ripping open the pack, he withdrew a grenade, pulled the pin and waited for the man to come closer. He heard the ladder creak as the man ascended.

It was time.

He tossed the grenade into the shaft, and it went off halfway down. A geyser of flame and smoke shot up out of the hole, followed by a rumble that shook the ground. The shaft was starting to collapse. Bolan rolled away from the hole as it started to grow larger, a slab of earth disappearing beneath his outstretched hand.

The earth shifted a bit as it settled, obscuring the shaft and leaving a broad funnel with no opening at the bottom. It grew very quiet.

Only then did Bolan notice the shadow on the ground beside him.

BOLAN REACHED for his side arm, but hands grabbed him before he could get the pistol out, hauling him to his feet. Half a dozen men pressed around him. Beyond them stood Kwanh.

"We have to hurry."

"What's going on?" Bolan asked.

"I'm not sure, but we have to get out of here. The Khmer Rouge are searching the tunnels. I don't know how they knew to look for us there, but they did." The

Vietnamese seemed preoccupied, as if something were tugging his attention away from the present.

"Where are we going?" Bolan asked.

Kwanh looked at him with a blank expression for a moment. Then, as if the question had awakened him from a deep sleep, he looked at the handful of men. He barked something in his native language, and three men lifted Bolan bodily and started running for the trees. Once there, he was placed on a stretcher with long handles. Two men stood in front and two behind. On a command from Kwanh they lifted. Kwanh took the point, and in moments the ruined village was a memory. The jungle closed around them with all the finality of a theater curtain after the last act.

But it wasn't the last act, and Bolan couldn't avoid confronting that reality. What had seemed so simple, so straightforward, was now as intricate as the shell of a nautilus. Every compartment led to another smaller one, on and on. There was no end in sight. But he had to continue, whether he wanted to or not. At the end Katherine May was waiting.

The men moved methodically without apparent strain. Bolan weighed more than two hundred pounds, but the stretcher bearers moved as easily as if the stretcher were empty. Kwanh kept glancing back at him, as if to make sure he was still there. Bolan wanted to sit up, but he knew it would just make the men's work harder. Prostrate, his weight was spread more evenly, and balance easier to maintain. He lay there, holding on to the edges of the stretcher, a thousand questions bouncing around his skull.

It occurred to him that the entire episode might have been an elaborate charade, designed and performed expressly for his benefit, but he was at a loss to explain what the point of such a complex deception might be. On the other hand, the timing seemed almost too perfect. Kwanh had gotten there just in the nick of time, like a Hollywood hero. It happened, he knew, more often than one might think. He himself had made such a last-minute arrival on more than one occasion. In a way it was what Bolan did with his own life, touring the world like some lethal Don Quixote, tilting at no less deadly windmills. But real life wasn't supposed to be so perfect, and it too seldom was.

So how did Kwanh get lucky? It wasn't the first time he'd asked the question, but he still had no answer.

The heat was taking its toll on the men now. Their clothing was soaked with sweat, and they breathed a little harder. They didn't appear to be suffering, but the work would quickly exhaust whatever reserves of energy they had. When it came, the collapse would be quick and total. Bolan only hoped they got wherever they were going before it came to that. The thought of having to walk on his bad leg was less than appealing.

There was no end to the questions, so he lay back and let his mind drift. After an hour Kwanh called a halt. The stretcher bearers set Bolan down gently, and the Vietnamese colonel squatted beside him. "Not far now."

"Where are we going?" Bolan asked.

"Someplace safe. That's all you need to know. That leg has to be looked at, and you need to rest."

"There's no time for that."

"Even you can't take on the world with only one good leg." Kwanh smiled distantly. "Fortunately for us we have allies in this part of Cambodia."

"I'll just bet you do," Bolan replied.

"You have to understand one thing. The people of Cambodia have been through more horrors than you or I can imagine. They don't like the Vietnamese, but they are realists. They remember what it was like when the Khmer Rouge were in charge of the whole country. They know that can happen again, and they'll do anything, even eat with the devil, to prevent it. If the devil happens to be Vietnamese, that's just the way fate would have it. But they won't turn away from a helping hand, no matter who extends it."

"You seem to be full of yourself this morning," Bolan observed.

"Not at all. But I know this part of the country, and I know many of the people. They'll help us. And make no mistake about it, we need that help."

Bolan didn't exactly agree with what Kwanh was saying, but he was too vulnerable to make an issue of it. As long as Kwanh was still amenable to working with him, he wouldn't push too hard. There was no way he was up to doing anything about it in any case, at least not for a few days.

He nodded, and Kwanh patted him on the shoulder. "Be patient. I want to find Katherine May as much as you do. I may have my own reasons, and those reasons are changing even now, but we *will* find her."

He got up and barked orders, once again in Vietnamese, and left Bolan wondering who these men were. They weren't dressed like soldiers, but the typical Cambodian peasant didn't speak Vietnamese, either.

A new team of stretcher bearers took over, and an hour later they entered a small hamlet. A dozen huts, all but one, the smallest, on stilts, encircled a small clearing. Beyond it plowed fields stretched out to a line of trees a half mile away. It looked like a thousand other villages he'd seen in Southeast Asia. The people chattered as the stretcher bearers moved across the open center of the village and set down their burden beside the small hut built at ground level.

Bolan realized this building was new. The thatching was still green and damp, while the others showed signs of being several weeks old. Kwanh spoke to one of the villagers, who pointed to the open field beyond the huts.

Kwanh nodded his thanks and started past the huts. Bolan got to his feet with difficulty, letting his good ankle take his weight. He watched the colonel make his way across the furrows, two of the villagers walking behind and to the left of him. One of the farmers in the field glanced up, waved a hand and passed the traces of his team to another man, then broke into a sprint toward the three approaching men.

Bolan watched their animated conversation for several minutes. Whatever was being said required much gesticulation. After the final spate of hand waving, Kwanh and the farmer started back toward the village.

Someone had given Bolan an aluminum crutch, its metal shaft stamped with the words World Refugee Council. He shook his head at the irony, then tucked the crutch under his arm. It was too short, but he could adjust the bolts and wing nuts to lengthen it. In the meantime it was good enough for him to hobble past the huts, where he stood waiting at the edge of the plowed field.

He glanced at the sky; the sulfurous color of the few scattered clouds was so familiar that he felt like a time traveler revisiting another century. Watching the farmers work with such primitive tools, while he leaned on a thin tube of metal strong enough to take his weight, he was forcibly made aware again of just how different this world was from his own, and just how great was the difference in their technologies. He knew, too, that that difference was reflected not just in the way people did their work, but in the way they thought.

Kwanh seemed more relaxed as he approached. The farmer beside him chatted nonstop in a rough-edged Khmer dialect, and Kwanh listened with one ear, occasionally commenting on the machine-gun monologue. The two small men stopped five feet in front of the much bigger American, Kwanh watching Bolan while he waited for the Cambodian to wind down.

When the farmer was finished—or at least pausing for breath—Kwanh put a finger to his lips, then turned to Bolan. "He says we can stay here for a couple of days. He can get someone to help with your ankle, maybe even some elastic bandage to wrap it. But he also says the Khmer Rouge are getting more active. He thinks something is about to happen. They're looking for someone, he says."

"Us," Bolan said matter-of-factly, and Kwanh nodded.

The Vietnamese said something to the farmer, who nodded, bowed and backed away. A moment later he was gone.

"I sent him for the doctor," Kwanh explained. "Not a doctor, really, but then it's a miracle anyone will admit to knowing anything at all about medicine. Apparently this woman was a medical student in France in the mid-seventies. Somehow she managed to survive the selective extermination. Now she tends to whatever illness she can with whatever comes to hand. Maybe it will help." He shrugged.

"The Chinese?" Bolan asked.

"No," Kwanh said. "The old man says they haven't seen any Chinese, but they've heard rumors. He doesn't know whether they're true or not."

"What did you tell him?"

"Nothing. I don't want to lie to him, but if I tell him the truth, he might get frightened. Better to say nothing."

The old man was back before they got to the ground-level hut, as it happened, built expressly for Kwanh and Bolan, since climbing a ladder would be all but impossible for the injured American. The woman in tow was younger than Bolan had expected.

Inside the hut she examined his ankle by lantern light, kneading the bruised and swollen flesh with gentle fingers. She poked and prodded to be sure of the full extent of the damage. When she was finished, she smiled.

"Nothing is broken, I think." Her English was halting, more from shyness than lack of facility. "You need to stay off it for a day or two and soak it in hot water. There are some herbs you can add to the water to reduce the swelling and help ease the pain. I'll tell Maranouk which ones. He'll find them."

She watched him closely to be sure he understood. When she was satisfied, she reached into a wicker bag and pulled out a soiled blue cardboard box. Opening it, she pulled out a length of elastic bandage. With her fingers she probed the box, then extracted two clips to hold the wrapping in place. "I'll need this back," she said. "It's the only one I have. And take it off when you soak the foot."

He looked at the frayed bandage for a moment. She took it back and began to wrap the ankle, handling the bandage as if it were worth its weight in gold. To her, Bolan thought, it was.

When she was finished, the woman spoke a few words to Kwanh, bowed gracefully and left.

Kwanh sat down beside Bolan. "I have much to do. Try to stay out of sight. I'll be back in the morning. As soon as you can move around again, we have a lot to do. In the meantime I'll make some arrangements. You'll have to be mobile by tomorrow. Can you do it?"

"Do I have a choice?" Bolan asked.

"What do you think?"

"I'll be ready."

Katherine May cowered in a corner of the abandoned temple. All around her lay the ruins of a once magnificent building. At the center of the now roofless building a pile of charred debris was half-covered with creeping vines, the green leaves fluttering in the early-morning breeze. They looked out of place against the mat black of the burned timbers. Beyond the mound of wreckage a huge stone Buddha lay on its back, its great stomach jutting into the air. It looked obscenely helpless, like an upended turtle.

Katherine had been raised a Buddhist. In any other circumstances she'd have been offended by the blasphemy, but she had more serious concerns at the moment. A night on the run had sapped her strength. Her clothes were torn and smeared with mud, her hair matted and full of twigs. She was hungry, she was thirsty, and more than anything else she was scared.

She'd heard them chasing her. Half the night they'd prowled around, often coming within yards of her. Once, one of them had been close enough so that she could smell the cheap cologne he wore. She still had the Browning, and her fingers ached from squeezing the grip through half the night.

But it had been more than four hours since the last close shave. When the noise of pursuit had faded, she'd held her breath for minutes at a time, convinced she'd been discovered and the silence was some cruel joke at her expense. But when nothing happened, no hand closed around her throat, no bullet smashed her skull, she'd permitted herself to hope.

At first it had been careful, tentative, not optimism so much as a diminishing pessimism. But when the seconds clicked away and still nothing happened, Katherine began to believe she'd done it, that she'd escaped. She wanted to shout in exultation but didn't dare. Slowly her confidence returned. For more than an hour she continued to squeeze the pistol tightly in her hand. Her fingers were so stiff that she had to pry the gun from her grip when she finally realized she didn't need it. Only then did she realize she'd actually managed to elude capture.

She sat there shuddering. Flashbacks of the terror, listening to the gunfire at night, watching people herded away, never to be seen again, seeing a familiar shirt worn by someone she'd never seen before, all crowded into her skull, the images jostling one another.

This was different, but worse in its own way. Then, at least, she had company in the horror, people at either shoulder, all seeing the same grisly sights, hearing the same terrible screaming. Now she was alone.

Sitting in the ruined temple, she felt like the last Cambodian on the planet. There was no one she could turn to for help, because there was no one she could trust. Not in the countryside. If she could get to Phnom Penh, she might get out of this alive. But could she make it?

Katherine was torn between the desire to run until her legs would carry her no farther and the horrible inertia that told her to sit where she was. And wait. To die. A picture flashed into her mind, then was gone almost as quickly. But its ghost lingered somewhere in her mind's eye, a pale afterimage, her bones in a heap, the skull sitting precariously atop the random pyramid of her skeleton, the eye sockets empty, except for shadows and the glittering shell of a beetle, flashing sunlit rainbows of color as it moved from one to the other.

She shuddered. That was her future if she stayed where she was. She wanted to deny it, to pretend that it couldn't happen, but if she stayed, she knew it would happen. And she knew, too, that she'd become that pyramid of bones, yellowing among the ruins of her culture, slowly crumbling to dust until no one on earth would know that she had ever existed.

She looked at the gun in her lap. It gave her no comfort. She slipped the safety on and tucked it into her pocket. Getting to her feet slowly, like an arthritic old woman, she straightened and shuffled her feet a moment before walking toward the prostrate Buddha. It wasn't until she had gotten to within a few feet of it that she realized it had been broken into a dozen pieces.

The whole figure looked like a great gray-green egg that had been sectioned. If it wasn't examined closely, it seemed whole and undamaged. But if time was taken to look at it, the destruction was evident. It must have cracked when it had been knocked down, shattering along hidden faults in the stone. It was like her country that way. No one had suspected it could come apart so totally, and so quickly. But it had.

And there was no way to put it back together again. Ever.

She shook her head sadly and leaned forward to run her fingers over the smooth stone. It felt warm, where the sun had been beating down on it and, for a moment, she thought she felt it move. It was nothing much, a faint throb, feeble but steady. It took her a moment to realize she was feeling her own pulse, her own blood pumping through her veins. And in that moment she realized there was no difference between the Buddha, Cambodia and herself. As long as one of them still breathed, still had life in it, however tiny the spark, they all had a chance to survive.

Katherine let her hand fall away from the shattered stone. She backed away a few steps and looked up at the sky. It was a clear and cloudless blue. She could hear the sound of the wind and the trees and, in the distance, a scolding monkey. Then another.

Suddenly a flock of parrots exploded up out of the canopy. Katherine knew her pursuers were drawing near. She ran toward a break in the ruined stone walls and slipped through the narrow gap.

Too late.

A man in a black uniform confronted her. He waved his assault rifle in the air, and half a dozen more men materialized out of the jungle. A moment later she was surrounded. She nodded her head once, then heaved a sigh as her arms were pulled roughly behind her and tied with thin rope. The cord cut into her wrists, and she bit her lower lip to hide the pain. The first man, a little taller than the others, and younger, frisked her, found the Browning and tucked it into his waistband.

The march back was unceremonious. Her captors weren't particularly rough, but they didn't much concern themselves with her comfort, either. It didn't take long. She was almost embarrassed at how little distance she had managed to put between herself and the camp. What had seemed like an eternity in the darkness the night before, a journey stretching from one end of the earth to the other, had in reality been less than three miles.

As she was marched back into the camp, the other prisoners, working with stony faces and dead eyes at their labors, scarcely glanced in her direction. She didn't wonder. She felt defeated herself, even crushed, and understood the despair that had reduced them to unemotional automatons. It was hard to care about anyone else when you didn't give a damn whether you lived or died.

Katherine was thrown back into her hut, the same stinking pesthole she'd hoped she'd left behind forever. The tall young man who seemed to be the leader of the detachment stood in the doorway. She couldn't tell whether he was watching her or simply waiting for his eyes to adjust to the gloom inside the hut.

She wanted him to say something to her. She didn't know what, didn't even really care. But a word, even an insult, would help her reestablish contact with the shrinking confines of her new reality. When she couldn't stand the wait any longer, she said, "I suppose I'll be seeing Comrade Phouma again?"

The young man laughed. She couldn't tell whether it was amusement or sarcasm. He didn't answer right away, and she was starting to grow uneasy. When he did speak, she knew why.

"Comrade Phouma is no longer with us."

"Where is he?" She felt a momentary sense of loss, then realized it was simply a loss of balance. She'd presumed that nothing would change. She'd come back, Phouma would chat with her briefly, then she'd be returned to her hut. She hadn't counted on this.

The young Khmer Rouge shifted his feet nervously as if he, too, were feeling disoriented by the change.

"Are you the new commander?" Katherine asked.

Again the young man laughed, this time bitterly. "I should be."

"But you're not?"

He didn't answer the question directly. He looked over his shoulder for a moment, then shuffled into the hut. "Comrade Phouma has been found to be a counterrevolutionary. He's been sent away to be re-educated."

Katherine felt a sinking feeling in her stomach. She felt as if she were responsible, as if her escape had caused Phouma's removal. She knew that was nonsense, that there was no rhyme or reason, and certainly no logic, to what passed for thinking in the innermost circles of Khmer Rouge power. Still, Phouma's fate seemed somehow connected to her, in a way she didn't understand but felt very deeply. The man had been almost kind in his treatment of her, compared to what she'd expected. And that, she realized, might be why he'd been removed. But she still felt there was a personal component. She knew it; she just couldn't explain why.

The young man had started to back out of the hut. She wanted him to stay. "Was it my fault?" she asked. "Was it because I escaped?"

The young Khmer Rouge shook his head. "No. It was because he was untrustworthy. He'd lost his faith in the revolution. He was poisoning the minds of his subordinates." It all sounded so logical that Katherine almost believed it made sense.

"And you?" she asked.

"What about me?"

"Was your mind poisoned?"

"Comrade Phouma was a good man. But good men sometimes make mistakes. They have to pay for those mistakes, pay more than one of which you don't expect so much. It was his failure. He'll have to learn to accept the consequences."

"Do you have any idea what those consequences might be?"

"He'll be reeducated, shown the error of his way of thinking."

Now it was Katherine's turn to laugh. "You think so?"

"Of course."

"You have a lot to learn, Comrade."

"I don't want to talk about it."

"You better think about it, though."

A voice barked somewhere across the camp, and the young soldier jumped as if he'd been stuck with a pin. "Come with me," he said when he recovered his composure.

"Where?"

"The new commander wants to talk to you."

"Suppose I don't want to talk to him?"

"That's up to you." He backed out of the hut. In the bright sunlight suddenly bathing his face, he looked even younger. Katherine followed him outside, and he turned sharply and marched toward the main building.

They entered Phouma's former office. The new man was seated behind the desk, facing a map pinned to the wall behind it. "That's all, Comrade," he said.

When the soldier had left, the new man turned in his swivel chair. Katherine gasped.

"Surprised?" he asked. It was Trang Van Leung.

10

"We have to wait here for moonrise," Kwanh said.

"You sure you can trust this man?" Bolan asked.

Kwanh seemed to mull the question over a bit before answering. "I'm sure we have no alternative. It's not the same thing, but it's as close as we can come."

The pagoda was a huge pyramid of ominous-looking shadows. From their vantage point on the edge of the jungle the temple looked deserted. Buddhism had all but been exterminated in most of Cambodia in the late seventies, and many of the temples had been torn down by the zealots under Pol Pot. That this one had escaped raised a few questions in Bolan's mind.

Kwanh seemed to sense his concern. "Something is troubling you?"

Bolan nodded. "I was just wondering how this particular temple managed to survive."

"I know what you're thinking. If Pol Pot left these monks alone, then perhaps he had a reason. Perhaps they were somehow useful to him, perhaps as spies."

"And?"

"I don't know. We'll ask the monk."

"If he shows up."

"Yes. If he shows up."

"And if he doesn't?"

"We'll have to deal with that the best way we can. I think he'll come. I was raised a Buddhist, and I still harbor a secret affection for the religion. That, of course, must remain our secret."

"Of course." Bolan lapsed into silence. The more he got to know about Kwanh the less he understood him. The man was a bundle of contradictions. He was extraordinarily intelligent, yet seemed strangely naive, especially in his politics. He was so gentle that it was difficult to understand him fighting alongside some of the ferocious warriors Bolan had encountered in what seemed now like another life. He wondered whether Kwanh found the same contradictions in himself, or if he was somehow able to compartmentalize himself and stay unaware of them.

The moon came up suddenly, and the pagoda seemed to come alive. Its burnished bronze roofs reflected the light, tinting the silver with a hint of gold. Intricate carvings covered all but the last tier. The massive building must have stood nearly three hundred feet. Its front footing was nearly as wide. Bolan couldn't see how deep the structure was, but guessed it must be a square. It was a breathtaking vision, rendered incongruous by the circumstances that had brought him here.

Kwanh, too, seemed in awe of the splendid temple. He glanced once at Bolan, as if to see whether the big man was as taken with the pagoda as he.

"We should go now," Kwanh finally whispered. "The monk will meet us in the courtyard garden." Before Bolan could respond, Kwanh stepped into the open and started toward the huge front doors.

The moon was behind them, and the massive portals, most likely covered in gold leaf, looked as if they were on fire. Kwanh bowed his head slightly as he started up the long tier of wide steps. The greenish-black stone was worn into a shallow bowl shape from a thousand years of use, millions upon millions of feet having tramped up and back down. The stairs were damp, as if they had recently been washed, and sparkled in the moonlight.

Kwanh stopped before the huge doors. He reached for the bell rope and was about to yank it when Bolan grabbed his wrist.

"Wait a minute, Kwanh. Try it first. No point in waking up everyone in the area if we don't have to."

Kwanh seemed offended. "It's tradition. Someone will escort us inside."

"We don't have time for tradition. Not now. The monks will understand. That's their job. Try the door."

Kwanh nodded, and Bolan let go of the man's wrist. The door on the right swung back easily, not making a sound. The colonel stepped inside, followed by Bolan. They were in a high-ceilinged vestibule. A pair of small oil lamps glowed on either wall, filling the room with orange light. Bolan pulled the door closed, bracing himself to stop it before it clanged against its mate.

Kwanh moved forward cautiously. Another, smaller doorway led into the dark interior. Incense swirled around them, and Bolan realized the lamp oil had probably been scented. For some reason he couldn't explain, he felt secure. It made no sense. The Khmer Rouge had no respect for any religious institution and would shell a temple like this one to rubble if they had reason to. Or if they didn't. The security was an illusion, but it was a powerful one.

The two men walked through a long, dark corridor until they came to another door, which Kwanh pushed open. A garden, surrounded by a high stone wall, covered nearly two acres. In the center a pool of water nearly fifty feet across was surrounded by low stone benches arranged in pairs.

The sweet fragrance of flowers was overwhelming. Bolan stepped out into the moonlight. The garden seemed to be deserted, but it was impossible to tell without searching through the tall clumps of flowering shrubs and the mazelike hedgerows. He felt as if he were committing a sacrilege as he shifted the safety on his M-16. The fire control was on semiauto. He changed it to full-auto as he sprinted toward the nearest clump of bushes.

It might be sacrilege, he thought, but it was better to be alive and sacrilegious than respectfully dead.

Kwanh didn't join in the search. Instead, he walked to the pool and took a seat on one of the benches. Bolan made a quick circuit of the wall. A single gate, its grillwork overgrown with vines, was set in the back wall, but it looked as if it hadn't been opened in a hundred years. Satisfied that the only way in was through the pagoda itself or over the wall, Bolan started to relax a bit.

He walked slowly toward the benches. Kwanh had his head bowed, almost as if he were praying. Bolan sat beside him on the bench without speaking. The Vietnamese looked up at him for a moment.

"This kind of peace. Why is it so elusive?" he asked.

Bolan recognized the question as rhetorical, and only nodded. The water rippled, and the Executioner looked at the disturbance in time to see a large carp flick its tail and slide though the tendrils of some lilies before disappearing. The water slowly became quiet again, the brilliant flash of the ripples dying out until the surface was as smooth as glass.

The warrior heard something behind him and started to turn. A hand touched his shoulder.

"It's all right," the man said in faultless English. "You're safe here."

Kwanh got to his feet, then bowed. "You're Chan Kong?"

The monk nodded. His saffron robes looked beige in the pale light, and Bolan thought of the Hare

Krishnas. How frenzied they seemed compared to the powerful serenity this man emanated.

"I don't have much time," Kong said. "Tell me what you need to know."

Kwanh looked at Bolan, nodded that the American should explain. The Executioner took a deep breath.

"An American citizen has been kidnapped. Her name is Katherine May and she works for the World Refugee Council. Her father is very influential in the American government, even though he was born in Cambodia. He has powerful friends, and there's considerable concern that she be returned unharmed."

The monk smiled. "But the Khmer Rouge don't feel the pressure, do they?"

"No, they don't," Bolan agreed.

"What do you wish me to do?"

"Help us find her."

"That's all?"

Bolan nodded. "That's all."

"I know where she was, but she's been moved. I don't know if I can learn where she's been taken."

"Do you know why she's being held?"

The monk nodded again. "So do you, although you didn't mention it. She's a courier for one of your intelligence agencies. I'm not certain which one, but in some ways they are all the same, aren't they?"

"How do you know she's been moved?"

"Because the man who was supposed to interrogate her has been moved from his command. He's been sent to a reeducation labor camp at Muong, not far from here. I believe he could help you if he's willing. I've seen such camps, and I'm sure he's willing. But it'll be difficult to get to him. It'll be a great risk."

"Who is this man?" Bolan asked.

"His name is Someth Phouma. He was in charge of the labor camp at Sisophon, where the woman was first taken. He has long been considered a counterrevolutionary malcontent. I don't know if there's a connection between the girl and what happened to him. I think maybe there is."

"Can you get us to Phouma?" Bolan asked.

"As I said, it'll involve great risk."

"We're prepared to take it."

The monk walked to the edge of the pool and dropped to a squat. For a long time he stared at the water, then leaned over to disturb the surface with a finger. "You see the ripples?" he asked.

Bolan nodded.

"One finger, here—" he plunged it into the water again, sending another series of ripples all across the surface "—and the water moves everywhere."

"I understand. You have my word that no one will know you are involved."

The monk considered the promise. He knew, as did Bolan, that there were no guarantees. Finally he straightened. "I don't worry for myself. But it won't affect just me. This temple has been here for more than a thousand years. Inside, there's a Buddha that was brought here from India. It belongs here now. Nothing should change that. But the Khmer Rouge..." He shrugged.

Watching him, Bolan was reminded of other monks, men with the same fierce determination hidden by a placid veneer. They had set themselves on fire to make a point. Chan Kong, too, had a point to make. The warrior wanted to say something to convince the monk, but he realized it was out of his hands. Kong would do what he wanted, for his own reasons. Whether he would divulge those reasons was doubtful. But Bolan understood that it didn't matter as long as he got to Phouma. He was the key to Katherine May's whereabouts. Without him they were stymied.

Finally Kong spoke again, this time in a whisper. "I'll do it. Wait here."

THE GUIDE WAS another monk, a young man whose shaved head glistened in the moonlight. After telling Bolan and Kwanh to stay close, he said nothing further. When the jungle closed around them, they could barely see him as he moved through the well-tended track. Creepers had grown across the trail, but the foliage on either side showed signs of having been recently cut back, as if it were regularly maintained.

Kong had told them that the reeducation center was in a converted pagoda about six miles away. Bolan's ankle was still sore, but he could use it reasonably well as long as he didn't have to run. It remained to be seen whether he could be that casual. Somehow he doubted it.

It took them two hours. By the time the young monk raised a hand, the moon was already beginning to set. From a low hill they could see the roof of the pagoda. It looked as if it had been neglected, perhaps even abandoned, before the Khmer Rouge had taken it over.

Getting to Phouma was going to be a problem. The prisoners detailed for reeducation were driven like human mules, often being hitched in threes to a plow and forced to prepare a paddy or cassava field for planting. Those who grew weak had their rations, meager enough to begin with, cut by two-thirds, guaranteeing they would get weaker still. The attrition rate was almost one hundred percent. Being sent for reeducation was in actuality being sentenced to death. Everyone knew it.

As they came down off the hill, they lost sight of the pagoda. The jungle was thinner here, but still thick enough to offer plenty of cover. The plan was for the monk to point Phouma out to them and then return. They'd then be on their own. Bolan knew the chances were slim, but the choice between slim and none was an easy one to make.

They waited at the edge of a partially plowed field. The pagoda was surrounded by small open-sided huts, and as the dawn approached, Bolan could see emaciated, ragged men moving restlessly under the badly thatched roofs. A half-dozen Khmer Rouge, in their black uniforms and red arm bands and headbands, moved mechanically among the huts. After a complete tour, they gathered in a knot and sat around a fire, passing cigarettes back and forth.

It was almost five when a shrill whistle echoed off the pagoda walls. The group of emaciated men spilled out of the huts and formed two ragged lines. The Khmer Rouge stood off to one side. Bolan saw a figure emerge from the pagoda and walk toward the double line of prisoners.

There were about fifty men in the two lines. Through binoculars Bolan examined them closely. Most of them were almost indistinguishable from one another. Sunken cheeks, arms and legs like sticks, skin covered with sores, they looked like something out of a bad zombie movie. But it was the eyes that struck him. They were extraordinarily large because the faces around them had collapsed inward. But they were lifeless. Like black marbles, they rolled in their sockets as the man from the pagoda walked back and forth in front of them, his arms folded behind his back.

Bolan was too far away to hear anything the man was saying, and he didn't speak any of the Khmer dialects in any case. Starting at one end, the warrior worked his way along, looking for a face less ravaged than the others. Phouma was a new arrival. He couldn't have been as emaciated. He'd had a prominent position until his recent disgrace, and he was supposed to be older, around sixty, with white hair. There were four candidates, but only one looked healthy enough to have eaten regularly anytime in the past few months.

He passed the glasses to the monk and directed him toward the right end of the back row. The monk nodded.

"That's Someth Phouma." He handed the glasses back to Bolan. The man turned and walked away. A moment later he was gone.

Bolan shook his head. Handing the glasses to Kwanh, he waited while the Vietnamese committed their quarry's features to his memory. When he was done, he let the glasses fall.

"We'll have to watch and see where he's working," Kwanh said. "We'll have one chance and one chance only. It looks as if the Khmer Rouge have been rearmed. When I was here last, only one man in six or seven had a rifle. Most of them had clubs. A rifle was a reward, something coveted even more than money."

"They treat their fellow countrymen worse than dogs."

Kwanh looked at him, seemingly surprised at the depth of Bolan's feeling. He opened his mouth as if to say something, then changed his mind.

"Maybe we can take out the guards and help them all escape."

"No!" Kwanh said. "We can't."

"Why not?"

"Because they have nowhere to go. They can't travel without papers. They'd simply be returned here. When it was found that they had escaped, they'd be killed." He handed Bolan the binoculars. "Look there," he said, pointing to the left of the pagoda.

Through the glasses Bolan could see an open pit. A mound of dirt in which several spades and mattocks had been stuck towered above it. Crows rose and fell in clouds over the pit. He lowered the glasses.

"What is it?"

When Kwanh spoke, his voice was taut. "That's the burial pit, where those men will end up, whether you try to free them or leave them here."

"But we can't just let it happen."

"We have no choice. You don't understand. When I came to this country for the first time, I came because I was a soldier and because we'd always hated the Cambodians, the same way they'd always hated us. It was a war, and I did what a soldier does in war. I killed my enemies. But when I left, I realized the Khmer Rouge were killing their own people in greater numbers than I could have dreamed of doing. I'm not an unsophisticated man. I studied in Europe. I've seen the films of the German concentration camps. They made me sick to my stomach. But this...this is..." Kwanh shook his head and walked away a few paces back into the jungle.

Bolan followed. "Dammit, Kwanh, we can't turn our backs on this. I *won't* turn my back on it."

Kwanh nodded. "All right. We'll have to wait until dark. In the meantime we wait and watch. We have to know what we're up against."

The surveillance was like a week in hell. Teams of three cadaverous prisoners stumbled along ahead of plows, a fourth guiding the blade from behind, turning up the rich earth in long furrows. The sun was merciless, and the men weren't allowed to take a break for water unless they got permission from one of the black-clad guards. More often than not a request was refused.

If a man fell, he was beaten with a bamboo cane until he got up. If he couldn't, which happened twice, he was removed from the traces and left in the sun to die. Watching at long range was torture. But Kwanh was right. They had only one chance, and they had better not make a mistake.

Well after noon another whistle sounded, and the men collapsed where they stood. Two more prisoners stumbled into the field lugging a huge pail. A third man passed out small wooden bowls to each of the prisoners. Some sort of pasty-looking gruel was ladled into the bowls by the two-man team.

Most of the men ate listlessly, as if they were too tired to eat, or as if the food were unpalatable. Bolan had seen enough similar situations to guess it was probably a combination of both. No more than fifteen minutes later the whistle blew again. The men went back to their plows while the mess crew gathered the bowls and tossed them into the pail. They stumbled back across the furrows and past the pagoda out of sight.

Bolan paid particular attention to Phouma. The man seemed to be in very good physical condition. He couldn't have been at the reeducation center for more than a couple of days. He worked hard, but even so, he was singled out by the guards. Twice he was pulled aside and lashed with the bamboo canes. The second time he fell to the ground. The man with the cane threw it aside and kicked Phouma twice in the ribs.

They were saving their most vicious punishment for him. Bolan wondered whether the man had once been on the other end of the stick, perhaps having commanded one of the guards, or done something to their families. Reports reaching the West were so sketchy that it was difficult to get a clear picture of the political structure of the Khmer Rouge. But it seemed to be a mindless tyranny of uneducated peasants who were suspicious of anything intellectual or authoritarian.

Government workers, doctors, schoolteachers, even simple soldiers in Lon Nol's army had been singled out and virtually exterminated. Now, it seemed, they were turning on one another because there was no one else to kill. But it was the people who were suffering; people who had never done a thing wrong were being brutalized by their own countrymen.

Watching Phouma through the binoculars, Bolan was getting a picture of the absurdity of it all. The men around Phouma were walking skeletons, men who had been rubbed away by the brutality scraping the flesh from their very bones and, when there was no more flesh to rip away, squeezing dignity and humanity itself from the hollow shells.

But he couldn't forget, couldn't allow himself to forget, that Phouma himself had been a part of the apparatus. It was like looking at Eichmann and trying to understand how so insignificant a man could have been responsible for administering so much horror.

Bolan didn't feel sorry for Phouma. He couldn't allow himself to fall into that trap. He had to recognize the man not only for what he was now, but for what he'd been mere days ago. He needed him, and that was an indisputable fact. And because he needed him, the Executioner would save him from being ground up by his own machine.

But he didn't have to like it.

Bolan watched Kwanh. The Vietnamese seemed even more withdrawn, as if what he'd seen here had squeezed the life out of him, too. Another contradiction. Here he was, in another nameless patch of Asian jungle, sitting next to a man who, at an earlier time, would have slit his throat. They were on the same side now, both trying to save the life of a man for different reasons. Who could figure it out?

11

Dusk finally descended. The agony of watching helplessly as people suffered was over. Bolan had spent the day watching mankind at its worst, and it made him heartsick. But he'd endured it all, knowing that this moment would come. Now it was here.

Kwanh, too, had turned inward. The man hadn't said a word since he'd agreed to the all-out assault. Bolan had watched him and seen him shrink away from the bamboo cane, sometimes so close they could hear it whistle as it arced through the air and landed with a horrible splat on its helpless victim.

Vengeance was called for, and the moment had come.

There were at least fifteen Khmer Rouge, possibly three more. Bolan had taken mental notes, letting each face burn into his synapses as if it were a branding iron. He'd kept the count, and he'd grown more angry with every addition. Now it was time to begin subtraction, setting the record a little closer to straight, bracing one arm of the balance against his broad shoulders and shoving it back nearer to level. It wouldn't help the three who had died in front of his eyes, and the countless dozens, perhaps hundreds, who had died in this godforsaken backwater. But it would make sure fewer died in the future.

For the moment he'd lost sight of Katherine May. But in the back of his mind he knew it was all the same. Whatever she had been here to do, he was helping a little. And he knew in his gut that he'd find her, and maybe finding her would somehow help Cambodia find itself again, help it recapture the spirit that had raised these pagodas, building monuments to a belief in something better than mankind, something higher, something purer.

They had about an hour before moonrise. Given the odds, they'd need darkness as an ally. And silence. As near as they could tell, a half-dozen guards were on night duty. The others were in the pagoda, probably sleeping. If he and Kwanh got that far, they wouldn't have to worry about noise. They could make enough thunder to shake the rafters of hell itself.

They crept along the edge of the forest, making their way to the ramshackle sleeping huts. A half-dozen fires burned throughout the camp. They smoked, probably to keep the mosquitoes at bay, but threw only enough light to drape shadows over the sleeping prisoners. Other, darker shadows glided quietly among the sleeping men. Occasionally polished metal would catch the glow from one of the fires and wink like a firefly once or twice as one of the guards made his rounds.

The two men needed a break, and Bolan kept his fingers crossed. They'd noticed during the day that whenever a man left the field to relieve himself a guard would accompany him. If they were lucky, they might take out one or two the same way. If not, they'd have to take more direct action.

When he was halfway around the plowed field, Bolan spotted a figure drifting away from one of the fires. He could tell by the shabby clothing that it was one of the prisoners. He watched the man tiptoe into the trees, then disappear. He seemed to have been heading in their direction, and Bolan pulled Kwanh into the trees to wait and see what would happen.

The furtive figure hadn't asked permission from any of the guards. Bolan was certain of that. If he was noticed, it might raise an alarm. The man flitted past them, moving quickly on his sticklike legs. As the prisoner moved past, half in a crouch, a club in his hand, Bolan held his breath. Whatever the man was up to, it had nothing to do with the call of nature. That much was clear.

When the man was out of sight, they moved on toward the pagoda. They hadn't gone more than ten yards when Kwanh grabbed Bolan's arm. "Look," he whispered, pointing at the middle of the field.

The warrior squinted into the darkness. At first he didn't see anything. Kwanh waved his finger impatiently, and the big man finally saw what the Vietnamese was pointing at. Three men, obviously Khmer Rouge, were inching across the furrows. Their path took them at an angle, and they were heading in the same direction as the prisoner who had just passed. When the men reached the edge of the field, they were no more than fifty yards away.

Bolan inched out of the brush. Far across the field, nearly at the tree line, he could just make out the prisoner, still in a half crouch, and moving quickly toward a stand of trees.

Beyond it, Bolan knew, was a field of cassava plants. He had noticed it earlier, and after he'd seen how ill-fed the prisoners were, wondered why no one seemed to be tending the plants. The tuberous roots were a staple of the Cambodian diet, and there was acre after acre of the plants just begging to be harvested. Yet it looked as if no one bothered with them. They had skirted the field that morning, and he'd seen no sign of any recent cultivation.

The prisoners seemed to subsist on rice gruel alone. Maybe the prisoner was sneaking off to gather a few of the roots to supplement his diet.

Using the field glasses, Bolan watched until the prisoner passed through the line of trees. Training the binoculars on the edge of the jungle, he picked out the three guards, moving more quickly now. It was obvious they were in pursuit of the prisoner.

This just might be the break they were hoping for. "Wait here," Bolan whispered.

"Where are you going?"

Bolan nodded toward the cassava field. "They just gave us a free pass."

"There's no time," Kwanh argued. "The moon will be up in less than an hour."

"I'll be back in twenty minutes."

"If you shoot them, the others will know we're here."

"If I get lucky, I won't have to shoot anybody," Bolan whispered. He indicated the bayonet on his hip. "And if I don't, it might just mean we're fresh out of luck."

Kwanh sighed with exasperation. "All right. But if you're not back in twenty minutes, I'm coming after you."

"If I'm not back in twenty minutes, you get the hell out of here. You go back to Thailand and get more help. Wherever Katherine May is, somebody's got to get her out. Somebody has to get to her."

"That's your job."

"Not anymore, Kwanh. I saw the way you watched those guards this afternoon. It's *our* job now, no matter what you want me to think."

Kwanh didn't bother to argue. Instead, he sank down into the lotus position and nodded. "I'll wait here. Twenty minutes."

Bolan barely heard him. He was already sprinting along the edge of the forest. The soft earth of the field made virtually no sound. He ignored the nagging pain in his ankle and pushed himself to the limit. Three minutes later he was at the tree line. He stopped to get his bearings for a moment, then pushed into the trees. A strip of jungle about fifteen yards wide separated the cassava field from the paddy. Two openings had been carved through the strip to give easy access, but the one nearer him was already beginning to be overgrown, further testimony that the cassava crop was being ignored.

Bolan eased through the opening, taking care not to get tangled in the thick, wiry creepers. The last thing he needed was to trip and fall, alerting the three soldiers to his presence. On the far side he sank to his knees and raised the binoculars. The head-high cassava plants offered someone in the middle of the field good cover. The three guards stood whispering to one another. They'd lost their prey and were arguing how to find him before he managed to get back to the camp.

After a minute, they split up, each man entering the ranks of cassavas about thirty yards from the next man. They didn't realize it, but they were giving Bolan the edge he needed. He waited until the last man had entered his row, then dashed across the open strip and angled along the edge of the field.

He had the bayonet in his hand, preferring not to waste the Beretta's ammo. He could see his target about twenty yards ahead. The man was tiptoeing through the open space between two rows of trees. His feet whispered on the stiff, dry weeds, enough to alert the prisoner if he was paying attention. But a hungry man probably would have his entire concentration on gathering the food as quickly as possible.

Bolan closed the gap, then ducked to one side as the man stopped and cocked his head to listen. He turned, but the Executioner was already in the next aisle. He knew the man wouldn't call out for fear of alerting the prisoner to his presence. When he heard the weeds whisper again, Bolan moved ahead, taking long strides and trying to time them to the halting steps of the Khmer Rouge soldier.

The noise, as soft as it was, grew a little louder, and Bolan sensed he was getting close. Maybe ten or twelve feet to go, he guessed. He shifted his grip on the bayonet and took two quick steps. Five feet and closing. Suddenly a cassava to his left bent into the aisle, and Bolan saw a leg poke through. He sprang as the Khmer Rouge shoved his body through, and slammed into the soldier with a shoulder. The man grunted, and Bolan clapped a hand over his mouth. The bayonet slid in between the man's ribs as he thrashed about. The blade found its mark, and the man's body suddenly sagged.

Bolan waited to make sure the man was dead. He tugged the blade free, stabbed it into the dirt to clean it and got to his feet. The aisles were about three yards wide. That meant he had to go through about ten or twelve aisles to get to the next guard.

The warrior sprinted ahead nearly a hundred yards, then started through aisle by aisle. After each one he stopped to listen. If he guessed right, he was ahead of his next target. But each aisle he crossed made it more likely that the Khmer Rouge guard would hear him.

As he pierced the eighth row, he heard the trees rattling a little to his right. Bolan moved closer, dropped to a crouch and waited, ready to leap at the first opportunity. A moment later the soldier sprang into the aisle. His face wore a broad smile, and in the near darkness it looked strangely sinister. When he saw Bolan, instead of the prisoner he'd been tracking, the man froze. The soldier backed away and opened his mouth to yell as the blade hit him in the gut. Bolan twisted the knife and reached for the man's throat, squeezing the larynx to cut off the shout.

He lowered the body to the ground, waiting for it to stop quivering. Standing upright, he listened for a long moment. Far down the row he heard the rustle of dry leaves. As he spotted the moving tree, it tipped to the side and lay across the aisle. Bolan raced forward, knowing he'd found either the prisoner or the sole surviving guard. Either way he wanted to be close enough to cut off a shout. As he neared the downed cassava, someone crept into the aisle on hands and knees.

It was the prisoner. He hacked at the base of the tree and jabbed his club into the ground. A moment later he was gnawing the root, not even bothering to wipe off the dirt. He heard Bolan's footsteps and turned. The warrior expected him to go for his weapon, but the man just froze. When the prisoner realized the man bearing down on him wasn't a Khmer Rouge, he got up and started to run.

Bolan closed on him in nothing flat. The man was too weak to run any distance. He caught him by the shoulder and clapped a hand over his mouth. A split second later the third soldier stepped into the aisle. His AK-47 was held at waist level. Bolan drew the Beretta and shoved the prisoner to one side as he dived to the other. In midair he got off two shots, both striking home. The Khmer Rouge guard backed up two or three steps, the Kalashnikov pivoting on his trigger finger as the weight of the gun carried his arm toward the ground. The Executioner fired a third shot, this one slamming the soldier onto his back.

Bolan turned to look for the prisoner, but the man was gone. He grabbed the AK and a spare clip and headed back.

THE PRISONER WAS GONE. Bolan hoped the man had made for the hills instead of running back to raise the alarm. It was unlikely the man would want to call attention to the three dead soldiers. It would be very difficult for him to explain how he just happened to be out for a walk after dark, and just happened to find three dead Khmer Rouge guards.

Bolan sprinted back through the cassava field to the tree line, stopping to examine the camp. When he saw nothing, he moved on through and into the paddy. He checked his watch—four minutes remained.

Kwanh was already on his feet when Bolan slipped back into the trees. The Vietnamese looked at him, but Bolan didn't waste time explaining. "Let's go."

They approached the pagoda on a run. Three Khmer Rouge still stood guard among the huts. Getting to them wasn't going to be easy, and they had to move fast. The longer they waited, the more restless the guards would become. Soon they'd be wondering where their comrades were and why they hadn't returned. How long did it take, after all, to chop a defenseless man to pieces, even if time was taken to cut out his liver first, as the Khmer Rouge were wont to do?

The three guards were strung out around the outer perimeter. One was dead center across from the pagoda. Beyond him were the sleeping huts and an open space, then the steps to the pagoda. The other two were on either wing. Crossing the open field was too risky. That meant one of them would have to circle behind the pagoda to get close to the guard on the far side.

Kwanh took the assignment. The camp was very quiet. Now and then one of the prisoners would moan, and the sound would drift across the open space and die away like the sound of a freight train whistle in the night. Signaling was impossible. They'd have to time it to the second.

Kwanh wanted ten minutes to get to the other side and get in position. Bolan watched him move off, then used the binoculars to check the immediate area around Phouma's hut. They'd have to get to him before they took the pagoda, because once the firing started, all hell would break loose. The prisoners would make a run for it, and if they lost Phouma now, they'd never find him again.

With three minutes to go Bolan turned his attention to the near-side wing man, lying on the ground and drawing his Beretta. The guard was about thirty yards away. The warrior wanted to get closer, but it was too risky. Sighting in on the back of the guard's head, he steadied himself and waited for the remaining two minutes to count down.

The guard was bent over something in his lap, but Bolan couldn't see what it was. He heard a rustling sound, then looked up to see another Khmer Rouge stepping across the open ground. The newcomer joined the seated guard, dropped to the ground alongside him and clapped him on the shoulder. They laughed softly, the sound obscenely inappropriate.

Metal clicked, then a spurt of flame appeared. The guards were lighting cigarettes. Bolan saw a little curl of smoke, and one winking red light as the new arrival turned to the side and dragged on his cigarette. Bolan held his breath. Thirty seconds. He hoped the new man stayed put. If he moved, he'd be far enough away to realize something was happening, but not close enough for the Executioner to get him before he shouted.

Fifteen seconds to go. The new man stood up and started to walk back toward the pagoda. At a comment from his confederate he turned back.

Five seconds. The new man was standing over his companion now, facing in Bolan's direction. He'd have to go first.

Bolan squeezed the trigger. The Beretta whispered its 9 mm message, and the bullet struck home with finality. The man crumpled, a collapsing shadow as the warrior shifted his aim and fired again. He caught the seated guard in the act of rising. He'd started to turn, and the slug smacked into his skull with the sound of a rock hitting a hollow stump.

The guard pitched forward, tumbling over the first target. Bolan was up and moving. He made a wide approach, moving away from the pagoda toward the middle of the paddy. When he reached dead center, he turned and sprinted forward. He could see the middle sentry, a shadow edged in pale yellow by the light from the fires. He was standing with his arms folded on his chest, his rifle slung over his shoulder.

The man must have heard footsteps because he turned in his tracks. Bolan hit the deck, saw the guard come forward a few steps, then heard him whisper. A flashlight came on, and Bolan aimed above and to the right. The light fell, landing on its end and sticking in the freshly plowed earth, its beam stabbing up at the night. Bolan scrambled to his feet and dashed forward, knocking the flashlight over and grinding it into the muddy ground.

Bolan headed toward Phouma's hut. He glanced toward the third guard but saw neither him nor

Kwanh. He hadn't heard anything and fervently hoped that Kwanh had pulled it off.

Picking his way past one of the fires, he nearly stumbled over a sleeping man—he'd taken the lump for a pile of rags. The man must have sensed something because he groaned, then tried to sit up. Bolan looked down into the man's eyes. They got bigger, and his mouth opened. The warrior clapped a hand over the prisoner's mouth as he started to shout, and held a finger to his own lips.

The man's eyes continued to bulge, but he nodded. Bolan relaxed the pressure slowly, waiting for the least sign that the man was going to raise an alarm. None came. Pulling his hand back, he watched as the man closed his eyes again, curled into a ball and went back to sleep. Breathing a sigh, the Executioner got back to his feet and skirted past another fire. The dense smoke choked him, and he suppressed the urge to cough.

Even with the fires the area swarmed with mosquitoes drawn by easy pickings. Bolan swept a hand ahead of him to disperse a particularly dense cloud. The odor of human waste and unwashed bodies was overwhelming, making the air feel thick and sticky. He breathed through his mouth to cut down the stench.

At Phouma's hut he looked back toward the third guard's position. Someone was heading his way, but he couldn't see. It was the right size and shape for Kwanh, and he crossed his fingers. The man drew closer. It was Kwanh. He, too, had taken a guard's AK.

The moon was already beginning to rise, a bubble of white just popping up over the jungle. There was no time to lose. Kwanh slipped into the hut and woke Phouma. Bolan could hear a whispered conversation. A moment later Kwanh was back, Phouma right behind him, the AK in his hands.

They moved toward the pagoda at a dead run. When they reached the broad stairway, Phouma grabbed Kwanh's sleeve and whispered something. Kwanh nodded, then said to Bolan, "There's always a guard inside the door. We'll have to take him out without noise to give us time to get to the sleeping quarters."

Bolan slipped the captured AK over his shoulder and fisted the Beretta again. He tilted his head toward the pagoda, and Kwanh started up the steps. Phouma joined him, then opened the door. Bolan stood to one side. The door swung open under Phouma's hand. The white-haired man leaned into the darkness and whispered something. A moment later a surly-looking Khmer Rouge guard stepped out onto the wide stone portico. He threatened Phouma with a club, waving it under the old man's nose. Phouma moved back a step, then another. The guard matched him step for step. When he was clear, Kwanh gave the door a shove, and it swung closed, Kwanh hanging on to the huge bronze handle to keep it from clanging.

Bolan slipped in behind the guard and snaked an arm around the man's neck. He lifted him off the ground and twisted the surprised man's head. A sharp crack broke the total silence. The guard sagged back against Bolan, who let him down gently, and tugged the body off to one side of the portico.

They were inside a moment later. Phouma led the way, his bare feet soundless on the smooth stone floor. They moved quickly through a narrow passageway, then turned right. The old man slowed and held a finger to his lips.

Another door, a smaller replica of the main entrance, blocked their path. Phouma opened the door a hair, and the muffled voice of a radio playing a rock song with Khmer lyrics drifted through the narrow opening. At least one man was awake.

Phouma closed the door, and the music vanished. Quickly, using his hand as a template, he sketched the layout of the room. It was a broad rectangle with a smaller room off one end, making it an ell. The sleeping quarters were at the far end. They had to get down there, or the Khmer Rouge would have some cover. The enemy was heavily armed and would fight fiercely.

Bolan wanted Phouma to stay in the passageway. If anything happened to the white-haired man, they'd lose the only link to Katherine May's whereabouts. But Phouma was adamant. He had a score to settle, he told Kwanh. Besides, he was a soldier and he wasn't as weak as most of the prisoners because he'd just recently arrived at the camp. Bolan gave in reluctantly.

Phouma moved back to the door and tugged it open slowly. The sound of the radio returned. Soft light spilled out into the passage, and the smell of spices and recently cooked food swirled into the darkness.

On three Bolan stepped through, his M-16 at his hip, Kwanh and Phouma right behind him. The Khmer Rouge guards were lounging around. Two men were playing backgammon almost directly in front of the warrior. One of the players sensed a presence and turned. He shouted just as Bolan opened up. He stitched both players, firing a tight figure eight. Leaping over the blood-spattered game board, he moved to the left and started down the long wall to get at the ell.

Men started shouting, and someone got his hands on a gun. A tight arc of tracer fire flashed toward the Executioner, and he dived to the ground. The bullets ripped at the wall behind him as he slid along the smooth stone. He fired short bursts from the M-16. Kwanh moved to the right, and Bolan caught a glimpse of him sprinting in a crouch.

All hell had broken loose as the Khmer Rouge scrambled for their lives. Two pockets of resistance developed quickly, one in the left-hand corner, dead ahead of Bolan. The other was in the mouth of the ell.

Bolan took cover behind a huge bronze urn. He held the M-16 in one hand, drilling two men who were racing for the ell. Three men in the corner pocket fired back. The slugs ripped into the urn, filling the high-ceilinged room with the sound of a tolling gong.

Kwanh was tucked in behind an open-topped stone cube that held a huge palm. He fired sporadically, picking his shots and conserving his ammunition. Phouma was prostrate in the center of the room, a cushioned divan providing some cover.

There was a lull in the firing, and Bolan noticed two men trying to slip out of the ell and creep along the wall. He fired two short bursts, nailing both, but one managed to toss a grenade as he fell. It bounced off the wall and fell into the urn. Bolan was up and running as the exploding grenade turned the urn into a cloud of swirling bronze knives.

Shrapnel sliced into his left arm above the elbow, and he felt a warm trickle of blood. The Khmer Rouge were getting it together. But they were too used to being in charge, and they got cocky. Four of them rushed Bolan, but he cut them down with a single snaking burst.

Kwanh took advantage of the opening to leapfrog to a second cube, closer to the ell. A second grenade arced through the air. Bolan caught it on the fly and sent it tumbling back toward the ell. The men positioned there left cover, all three of the attackers opening up.

Bolan grabbed a new clip as a man charged straight for him. He lost his grip on the clip, and it danced away over the smooth stone. The man started firing, and the warrior rolled to the left, narrowly avoiding the deadly hail of gunfire.

Phouma stuck out a leg as the man rushed past, and he went down hard. Bolan had the Beretta out and snapped off a quick shot. The soldier slid headfirst into a stone step, his skull cracking loudly on impact.

It took Bolan a moment to realize that it was all over. The pagoda was full of silence. And the smell of cordite.

12

Bolan stood in the doorway of the pagoda. The huts were blazing, and the camp was deserted, except for one man. As he stood and watched the flames consume the rude huts, he heard an engine start. A moment later the pagoda was flooded with light. Someone must have started the generator. He turned back to the huge doors that yawned open and watched Phouma and Kwanh walk slowly down the long passageway toward him.

When they reached the open door, Phouma stepped out onto the smooth stone portico. He let his rifle slide to the ground and heaved a great sigh. He said something to Kwanh, who looked at Bolan. The big American nodded, and Kwanh translated. "He says he never thought he'd live to see this happen."

"We have to get out of here," Bolan said. Kwanh agreed, then explained to Phouma.

The Cambodian said, "I speak English." He smiled sadly. "I never let anyone know. That would have been certain death for me and my family."

Kwanh tugged at Phouma's sleeve. "Come on, then."

Phouma nodded, then walked down the wide stairway and turned to look back up at the pagoda's tiered roofs. He was crying, and brushed absently at the tears with a filthy sleeve. Then, as if nothing had happened, he turned his back. "Follow me."

The Cambodian led the way into the jungle. The moonlight was blocked by the trees lower down, but up above clouds were lit as they scudded by on a high wind. Bolan turned to look back. The dense black smoke from the burning huts thinned as it climbed, turning to a pale haze, then disappearing altogether. He wondered whether it was just rage or a desire to cleanse that had led the prisoners to burn the huts. But in the end it wouldn't matter why. The effect would be the same.

Phouma hadn't stopped, and Kwanh was lagging a little behind him to make sure Bolan didn't lose them. The big man broke into a stiff-legged trot. His ankle throbbed a little, but he felt good, as if something had been accomplished that couldn't be undone.

After an hour the pagoda was just a memory, and Bolan was able to focus on the job ahead of him. He wasn't certain he could count on Phouma to help him. The farther from the pagoda they moved, the less the ugly memory of his captivity would bother the Cambodian. That he'd want to help was by no means certain. That he *could* help was less certain still.

But Kwanh had confirmed that Phouma knew about Katherine May and where she was being held. He'd also hinted that there was more to it than Bolan suspected. He'd promised to explain once they found refuge. They were heading deeper into Cambodia, but Phouma insisted they had to get away from the northwestern corner, where the Khmer Rouge still controlled much of the land.

The nominal government on Phnom Penh was anything but secure and had virtually no army to speak of. Instead, the country had been carved into a series of petty fiefdoms, each under the control of a different group. The Khmer Sereikar held the southern part of the Thai border, the Khmer Rouge the northern part. Much of the rest of the country was dominated by warlords, the way China had been well into the twentieth century.

When they reached their destination, Phouma wanted to bathe and change his clothes before talking any more. They had reached a small village, which Phouma insisted was secure. Many of the people were still so frightened of the Khmer Rouge that they went to pieces as soon as they saw someone in the black uniform. If the Khmer Rouge entered the village, Bolan and the others would most likely be compromised. But it was a chance they would have to take.

Phouma took them to a hut and introduced them to an old man who he said was a cousin of his mother's. The old man and his daughter, who herself was Phouma's age, offered them food. The old man then led Phouma to a public bath where he could soak the filth of the camp out of his skin and bones.

While they waited for him to return, Bolan and Kwanh picked at some cassava and rice. Kwanh seemed nervous about something, and Bolan waited for the woman to leave them alone before asking him about it.

"I don't know," Kwanh said, "whether we should trust him. Maybe we should just find out where the girl is and go our own way."

"I was thinking the same thing. But we can't decide that until Phouma tells us more. We might need not only his but other help, as well."

"You still have that code book, don't you?" Kwanh asked.

Bolan nodded.

Kwanh looked grim. "Because I have a feeling we're going to need it before this is over."

"That's what Salang thought."

At the mention of the dead lieutenant Kwanh shook his head. "I still don't know how they knew we were coming, and where we were going to be."

"The jungle's full of secrets," Bolan said, "but not all of them are well kept. I remember once in your country, we were moving in on a village suspected of being a hotbed of VC activity. Our intelligence people had been getting information from all over the place. It all jibed, and we were told to take a closer look. But—"

"It was deserted when you got there, wasn't it?" Kwanh said. He could barely disguise the beginning of a tiny smile.

Bolan nodded. "Yeah, it was deserted. We figured somebody must have tipped the VC off, because we'd been very careful."

"Information always has a price. We knew that as well as you did. It was always possible to buy enough information. But you have to know what the price is. That was one thing you Americans never learned. It wasn't about money, or sex, or even food. More often than not it was about pride, pride in your people, in your country. You were the outsiders, and everyone knew you. They could spot you a hundred miles away, they could see you coming, and since they knew what you wanted, it was easy enough to give it to you. Keeping it was your problem."

This time Kwanh did laugh. "Now we're both outsiders. As much as the Cambodians hate the Khmer Rouge, they hate foreigners more. Thais, Americans, Chinese, Vietnamese, Laotians. It doesn't matter. We're all outsiders. Right now the Chinese are tolerated by the Khmer Rouge because they're the only ones willing to send assistance. But that won't last. The people welcomed us as liberators when we first came. But as soon as the Khmer Rouge faded in their memories, they were fed up with us. They wanted us to leave. Finally we had no choice. That's a lesson we've both learned."

"Maybe so," Bolan said. He knew there was an element of truth in what Kwanh had said, but he also knew that generalities seldom explained everything. There was another factor here, one both he and

Kwanh had overlooked. He couldn't put his finger on it, but he'd be willing to bet that Phouma knew. Whether he would tell them was another matter.

Phouma returned, looking cleaner but no more rested. He folded his legs beneath him and sat down to eat. The old woman was back, thrusting a bowl of rice into the Cambodian's hands, then backing out, as if he were too good for her to be in the same room.

He ate greedily but still managed to maintain some sense of decorum. Bolan watched him, convinced that Phouma was no ordinary Khmer Rouge. There was too much breeding in the man's background. He seemed sophisticated, almost regal.

When he'd taken the edge off his hunger, Phouma let the bowl rest in his lap. He looked at Kwanh for a long time without speaking, then turned to Bolan and asked, "So why did you come to my rescue? Surely my welfare was no concern of yours. What exactly do you want?"

The question was directed to neither man. It hung in the air like an invisible cloud. Kwanh nodded at the Executioner.

"There's a woman, an American citizen. We have reason to believe you might know where she is."

Phouma nodded. "I thought there was something unusual about her. It seems I was right about that."

"Do you know where she is?"

"Miss May? Is that who you mean?"

Bolan waved the question away. He was getting impatient. Phouma sensed it and shook his head slowly.

"Of course it is. I know where she was a few days ago. Now I don't know. But I can find out."

"Was she all right?"

"She hadn't been harmed, if that's what you mean. But I know she was going to be questioned by one of our more zealous interrogators, a man not noted for his delicacy."

"If you locate her, can you take us to her?"

Phouma shook his head. "Impossible."

"It's important."

"Tell me why. Perhaps I was wrong about her."

"Her father is very influential in American business circles and has friends in high places. There's some expectation that he'll represent American interests in negotiating a new government for Cambodia."

Phouma laughed. "New government? Ridiculous. This place is ungovernable. There are two dozen factions scattered all over the mountains and the jungle. Cutthroats in every one of them, too. Each is led by a man who thinks he ought to head the government, and none will agree to anything less than total control. Add to that the interference of the Chinese, the threat of another Vietnamese invasion, and the specter of the American B-52s, and you have a recipe for permanent chaos. Your governments brought it on. And now you care about one woman when ten million weren't accorded the concern one would give a dead fly?" Phouma shook his head as if he couldn't believe what he was hearing.

"I don't care about ancient history," Bolan said. "I just want the woman back."

Phouma ignored him, his eyes boring into Kwanh's for a long moment before asking, "And what is this woman to you?"

Kwanh shrugged.

Phouma sighed. "So it seems I was wrong. She is a spy after all."

"No, not a spy," Kwanh said. "Not even a courier really. But we know she was to contact one of our agents, a man who was killed within a few hours of her kidnapping. All we're really interested in doing is offering whatever small assistance we can to the Americans. The world is getting smaller. We all know this. And the war has been over a long time now. Some in my government think it's time we got on with our lives, and that our countries learn to live together."

"Very pretty words. I don't believe a single one of them."

Kwanh started to answer, but Bolan beat him to it. "Look, I don't care about any of that. Will you help us find the woman, or won't you?"

"What's in it for me?"

"A new life."

"Ah," Phouma said. "I see we have more than one language in common."

"Will you do it?"

"If I can learn where she's been taken, I'll decide. That's all I can say at the moment."

It wasn't much, but it was all Bolan had.

THEY WERE WAITING for news, and waiting wasn't something Mack Bolan did well. He paced, trying to walk off his irritation. He, Kwanh and Phouma had spent two hours cleaning their weapons, packing ammunition and making sure they were ready to leave at a moment's notice. But it had been hours, and the notice hadn't come.

Phouma claimed to have information not on Katherine May's location, but on the whereabouts of someone who might know where she'd been taken. He'd tried to explain how the Khmer Rouge were ripping at one another like sharks in the first stages of a feeding frenzy, but Bolan couldn't care less about the internal squabbles of a bunch of butchers. He wanted to know where Katherine May was, and what he had to do to get her back. Anything else, as far as he was concerned, was hot air.

But Phouma pointed out—and Kwanh agreed with him—that they were picking their way through a minefield. One mistake was all they'd get the chance to make. Phouma argued that they had to proceed step by step, always checking where they were, figuring their next move and the one after that.

Since that was the way Bolan had always worked, he had to muzzle his impatience. Phouma was right, but it still didn't sit well with him. Seeing the work camp to which Phouma had been taken had set his teeth on edge. He knew that the entire fabric of Cambodia was tearing apart at the seams. It wouldn't take much for

Katherine May to be torn to pieces right along with her homeland.

By nightfall, when there still had been no word, Bolan was ready to break a few eggs. He was tired of tiptoeing through the pettiness and the tender feelings, the ethnic animosity and the political paranoia. He sat down across from Phouma, who was trying to control his own anxiety. Kwanh watched quietly from a corner of the hut. He was the only one who seemed to be in complete control of his emotions. Bolan didn't know whether to envy Kwanh or wonder what was wrong with him.

Patience had been the critical factor in the Vietnam War, but it wasn't until now that he understood just how patient the Vietnamese were prepared to be. Controlled to the point of catatonia, Kwanh moved little and said less. Instead, he contented himself with a walk to the latrine and back. Twice. In sixteen hours.

"Where the hell is he?" Bolan snapped. His voice was taut with the suppressed tension, the words cracking off the walls like small stones.

Phouma shrugged. "He'll be here soon. I don't know precisely when. It's dangerous work he's doing."

Bolan stood again and walked to the door of the hut. Outside, the village was slowly winding down the day's work. A handful of people were out in the open spaces before their huts, preparing meals over small fires. The only noise was whispered conversation between the women as they worked on the meals. The children were indoors, the men, exhausted, either already asleep or waiting to eat.

At nine-thirty Bolan heard the whine of an engine. It was a jeep, and it had to be Phouma's man. No one else in the village had a vehicle, and no one else in his right mind would be abroad after dark unless it were an emergency.

He sprinted to the narrow road that led into the village, swelled like an aneurysm around the camp, then constricted again to continue off into the silent jungle on the other side. He could see the gleam of a single headlight. It was askew, and speared up and to the right. It rose and fell arhythmically as the jeep lurched over the pitted dirt road.

Phouma and Kwanh must have heard the engine, too, because they joined him at the mouth of the road.

The old man patted the warrior on the arm. "Let's hope Bopha has the information we need."

Bolan didn't even want to consider the possibility that the man wouldn't. He watched the jeep with its skewed, cyclopean eye barrel toward him through the darkness. When it slowed to enter the village, he stepped aside and waited with one hand on the overheated hood while the driver shut the engine off and climbed out. Phouma leaned in from the other side, obviously more impatient than he'd let on.

The driver, sensing the urgency of the men who bracketed him like nervous bookends, started to tell Phouma what he'd learned. Phouma halted him with a raised hand while he translated the first part. "He says he found the woman. That she's in a work camp. He couldn't get close enough to ask her anything."

"Ask him," Bolan demanded, "if we can get her out alone."

Phouma translated the question, and the man shook his head.

"Find out where it is," Bolan instructed. "We'll get her out."

Bolan tapped his fingers on the hood while Phouma grilled the anxious driver. When he was done, he nodded toward the hut. As the warrior turned, he saw Kwanh in the doorway, outlined by the glow of a small oil lamp, the only source of light in the village huts.

Inside, Phouma explained the situation to both men. Kwanh didn't seem surprised, nor did he seem reluctant to take the next step. Looking at Bolan, he asked, "We go tonight?"

"You bet."

"We have to think this through," Phouma cautioned.

"We're done thinking," Bolan argued. "We have to move. We can talk this thing to death, but we need to move as soon as we can."

Phouma sighed. "You're right, of course."

"Look," Bolan said, "if you want out, just say so. No hard feelings. Tell us where and we'll take care of it."

"No. She's in this situation because of me. I'll help get her out."

"If you're sure..."

"I'm sure."

"Then let's go."

The Executioner sprinted to the hut and grabbed his rifle and pack. Kwanh and Phouma were right behind him, lugging their own gear. The decision to move seemed to be something that each man had waited for in his own way but wanted no less than the other two. Bolan knew it was going to be rough, maybe even impossible, but standing around waiting had never been preferable to acting. Better to give it your best shot, he thought, then worry about whether it would be good enough.

They were taking the jeep, and as Bolan reemerged into the center of the village, the driver had just finished refueling it. He set the second of two five-gallon cans on the ground and nodded. He said something Bolan didn't understand, then stepped forward and extended his hand. The warrior took it in his own, and the little man patted the back of Bolan's wrist with his free hand. He bowed and backed away as Kwanh climbed into the jeep.

The Executioner took the wheel and cranked up the engine while he waited for Phouma. All of his energy was focused on the job ahead. He looked at the village. People were in the doorway of every hut. As he kicked the gearshift into first and gunned the accelerator, the people waved.

There was no love here for the Khmer Rouge and no respect, either. Only fear. The people were pulling for them, not because they cared about Katherine May—

even if they knew about her—but because anything that hurt the Khmer Rouge was some small payback for years of misery and torture. Most of those in the little village had lost half of their families. They wanted vengeance, and they were on the side of anyone willing to exact some small measure of it.

As the jungle closed around them, Bolan looked at Phouma, sitting in the passenger seat beside him. "How far?"

"Not much more than sixty kilometers," he said. "Maybe seventy. But we'll have to walk the last three or four. There'll be guards, and the jeep makes too much noise."

"Do you know the layout of this camp?"

Phouma seemed reluctant to answer. "Yes...I know it."

"You know it well, don't you?"

Phouma nodded. "Yes, I know it well."

Bolan knew how much it cost the Cambodian to admit the truth. He must have been commander of the camp at one time. There was no other explanation for the emotion he was choking back. But that was another chapter of ancient history, as far as Bolan was concerned. It wasn't up to him to pass judgment on the man. That would be for the people of Cambodia.

But not just yet.

The old jeep was loud, the steering was loose to the point of being wobbly, and Bolan had to wrestle the wheel constantly with both hands to keep it more or less in the center of the makeshift road. He had the feeling it was being guided as much by the deep ruts as by any effort of his. The one working headlight was almost useless, showing him a great deal of the upper canopy of the forest and casting only a pale secondary swatch of light onto the surface of the road. But it was too dark to see without it and would be until the moon came up.

Bolan was aware of Kwanh's silence. The Vietnamese sat in the back seat, an AK-47 across his lap. The warrior glanced back and saw the man's small fingers curved protectively around the trigger guard. He wondered what was going through Kwanh's head. There were still some unanswered questions, questions he'd wanted to ask but had pushed aside as too delicate. But before this was over he wanted to know the answers. Who had set the assassins on them in Bangkok? Who had engineered the ambush? Who was responsible for the death of Lieutenant Salang?

Bolan thought these same questions were tormenting Kwanh, but the man had the key to the answers. Bolan wanted the key, and he meant to have it.

Soon.

The men remained quiet as they drove deeper into Khmer Rouge territory, straining to hear above the roar of the unmufflered engine, listening for the least indication that someone had spotted them.

Bolan kept his eyes on the road as best he could. When the moon slipped up over the canopy, making the dark shapes of the trees darker still, he clicked off the nearly useless headlight. On either side a wall of black trees pressed in on the jeep and its occupants. It reminded the Executioner of those old movie serials where the walls moved toward each other and at the last second the hero managed to stop them by jamming a metal pipe between them, leaving just enough room for him to breathe.

The jeep's odometer was broken, and they were relying on Phouma's memory to gauge the distance. There was only the one road, with a single intersection so far, so they hadn't gotten lost, but Bolan was worried that they'd come across the Khmer Rouge before they knew it. Even two kilometers might be too close with the jeep's rusted-out muffler making more noise than a nitro-burning dragster.

Bolan had tried to hold the speed steady and had managed to keep the needle somewhere between fifteen and twenty kilometers per hour. After three hours on the road, they had to be getting close. Phouma kept leaning forward to stare ahead of them, looking for some sort of landmark. They'd passed a village, set off the road to the left, but it had seemed deserted, and Phouma didn't know its name in any case. Villages were almost as impermanent as a small clearing hacked in the jungle, and seemed to grow up as fast and die as easily.

They were heading northeast now, leaving the relatively free zone around the Tonle Sap far behind. Somewhere beyond their destination was the Thailand border, but there was a lot to be done before they needed to concern themselves with that.

Bolan was about to ask Phouma if they were getting close when they came to another intersection, though the road that cut across theirs was barely worthy of the name. The Cambodian reached out and grabbed the wheel. "Stop!" he hissed.

The Executioner backed off the gas and let the jeep coast to a halt. Phouma jumped down and leaned toward the jungle. He seemed to be peering at something. Bolan followed the older man's gaze and, so faint he almost missed it, he saw what the Cambodian was looking at. Bleached to a silver gray, its hand-painted letters almost flaked away to nothing, was a road sign. Phouma approached it cautiously, then fanned his palms together in silent applause.

He climbed back into the jeep. "That's it. Sisophon three kilometers. Find someplace to leave the jeep."

A hundred yards back Bolan had seen a small clearing scooped out of the jungle, and he eased the transmission into reverse. The gears ground once, then engaged, and the jeep moaned backward. When he found the spot he was looking for, Bolan jerked the wheel and backed the jeep all the way off the road. It lurched through a shallow ditch but kept on moving. When he had the tail up against a thick-trunked tree, he killed the engine.

Kwanh was already out of the jeep, whacking at some tall fronds. He started to drape them over the jeep while Bolan and Phouma unloaded their gear from the back seat. When Kwanh was finished, he had fashioned a passable thatching of camouflage that would conceal the jeep but take only seconds to remove should they need to get out in a hurry.

"We take the road on foot until we get closer," Phouma said. "There'll be a small guard deployed on the road. The camp is off to the left."

"How heavily defended?" Bolan asked.

"Twenty men, maybe a few more."

"It doesn't make any difference," Kwanh said. "We'll get Katherine May out if there are fifty men."

Bolan caught the little man by the shoulder. "No showboating, Kwanh. You've had an ax to grind since this thing started. I don't know why, or what it is, but

I'm warning you—we can't screw this up. Understand?''

''Better than you think,'' Kwanh replied. His face was empty of emotion, almost serene. It was frightening because it seemed so benign. Bolan let go reluctantly. He wasn't convinced he'd made his point but didn't know what else to do. He would have to watch his back, and Phouma's, and keep an eye on the Vietnamese, all at the same time.

He backed up a step, then turned on his heel and started down the road. Kwanh fell in beside him almost immediately and tapped the warrior on the back. ''I wish I could tell you more,'' Kwanh said. ''But I can't. You'll just have to accept that.''

''I don't have to like it, though.''

''No, you don't. But you can trust me. Please try to believe that. It might make a difference to all of us.''

Bolan looked sidewise at the smaller man. Kwanh's expression was almost pleading, and it was the most emotion he'd ever seen Kwanh display. If he was acting, he was doing one hell of a job.

The Executioner let out a long, slow breath. ''All right.''

They covered the first kilometer and a half at a dog trot, but as they shrank the distance between themselves and the camp, they settled first into a fast walk and then a cautious one. There was no way for any of them to know what lay ahead, and no way to control what was about to happen. In that respect, at least, they were all equal.

The last kilometer they took by leapfrogging turns. Every hundred feet or so Bolan would hold them back and scan the road ahead. Since the road to the camp was on the left, they were moving down the left edge of the jungle. If Phouma was right, two or three men would be just a few meters down the side road at the cutoff. There would be no way to see the sentries until they were almost on them. The small side road itself would be all but invisible, even with the aid of the moon.

If they were right, the cutoff should be no more than a hundred and fifty to two hundred yards ahead now. Bolan was the point man. He clutched his Beretta tightly in his right hand, ready to cut loose with a tri-burst at the first sign they'd been discovered.

At fifty yards Bolan held up a hand. He thought he heard something, possibly a voice, and he listened intently, waiting for it to be repeated. After three minutes of total silence he heard it again. The sound was muffled, a soft murmuring. He still wasn't sure whether it was a voice, or just a rustling of leaves.

He shifted the fire control on his Beretta, setting it to single shot. Better to take his time and aim carefully, save ammunition. He inched forward a dozen yards. He heard the noise again, this time echoed by another, deeper muttering, similar but no more intelligible.

Conversation. It couldn't be anything else. Bolan crept closer, after signaling that Kwanh and Phouma should sit tight. He struggled through a tangle of thorny veins strangling the edge of the jungle. He could hear the conversation more clearly now. There was no doubt. Two men for sure.

Bolan was within ten yards before he saw the first man, a lanky kid in the typical black uniform. The guard's shadow spilled away from him, a charcoal stain on the dirt road tinted silver by the moon. He was looking down the road, probably toward the camp. Bolan watched patiently, waiting to see if the guard had been one of those speaking. If not, that upped the tally to three.

Bolan heard another exchange, somewhere off to the left of the man he could see. Three it was.

At least.

The two men behind him couldn't use their guns without rousing the whole contingent of Khmer Rouge. If there was any shooting at all, it had better come from the Beretta. That meant he had to make sure on each shot, perhaps as many as three, before the other side got off a round.

Bolan didn't want to fire the first shot until he had visual contact with all three men. He had to get closer. Keeping his eye on the one man he could see, he moved away from the tree line a couple of yards, just enough to give him an angle. He kept the Beretta trained on the one target he had, hoping he didn't have to fire until he was ready.

Suddenly he heard tinny music, the sound of a cheap radio. The guard he could see said something. Bolan heard a click, and the music died as suddenly as it had been born. Someone grumbled and the guard snapped again. This time someone moved out of the shadows. The new man confronted the first guard. He was smaller and jutted his chin forward and up as he argued, obviously with his superior.

Another shadow detached itself from the trees and joined the argument. Bolan drew a bead, waiting to see whether anyone else joined the dispute. When he was convinced there were only three men, he squeezed the trigger, taking the tallest of the three in the side of the head. The guard went down and the other two spun in panic. Neither had his rifle in hand, and Bolan fired again. There was a groan, and one of the two men staggered. Wasting no time, the Executioner let loose a third shot as the remaining guard raced back to the trees. The round caught him in the shoulder and he stumbled but kept running. Bolan was moving now, and he heard Kwanh and Phouma rush forward.

Once in the open the warrior dropped to one knee, aiming carefully as the last guard found his rifle. The 9 mm slug found its mark, and the man went down without a sound. When Bolan straightened, Phouma already had the wounded man in his grasp. He fired questions and the guard—little more than a youth—kept shaking his head, as if he didn't know what Phouma was talking about.

In disgust Phouma shoved the youth to the ground. Kwanh drew his bayonet and put an end to the whimpering.

There was no time for anything else.

BOLAN DECIDED it was time to use the code book. The chopper would have to be there when they were ready, but not a moment before. He figured a two-hour flight, given the distance to the border. If it took an hour to set up the attack and another hour to execute, get Katherine May out, and get ready for the pickup, it would work. But if they hit a snag, the chopper wouldn't be able to hang around.

As it was, it would be a violation of Cambodian airspace, not that Bishop and his kind gave a thought to such trivialities. Nor, for that matter, did Bolan. But it meant that things had to work like a Swiss watch. If not, the fan would start turning, and God only knows what would hit it.

Bolan stepped into the trees and was joined by Kwanh, a small flashlight ready in his hand. He worked out the code, flipping through the pages impatiently until he found what he needed. Each code was a couple of lines from a poem. What he needed was the code to tell Bishop's people they wanted a pickup, that Katherine May was with them alive and well, and that urgency was a priority. After sifting back and forth through the cluttered pages, he found what he needed.

Now all he needed was to raise somebody on the other end of the line and give them a required ETA. That was how it was supposed to work. He crossed his fingers and committed the lines to memory. Then he shoved the book into his pack. He thought about trashing it. It was flash paper and would go up like a phosphorous flare, but in the back of his mind was the thought that he might still need it.

He pulled the small transmitter from his pack and clicked it on. Kwanh watched quietly, occasionally glancing toward the clump of undergrowth from where Phouma was watching the road to the camp. Bolan tried twice to raise someone on the other end, but all he got in return was static, and not much of that. He tried a third time and got lucky.

"Eagle Nest here. That you Bird One?" The voice was faint, but it was audible.

"Bird One, roger, Nest."

"Got a poem for me, One?"

"Roger that." Bolan recited the two lines.

"Not my favorite poem, One, but I'll pass the word. Out!"

"Let's go," the warrior said.

This time they didn't want to use the road. It was little more than a pair of ruts, and they couldn't risk being spotted. Too many times Bolan had seen somebody get himself killed by letting out a little too much slack once he'd made the first move. But that wasn't his way, and he wasn't about to start it tonight.

After fifteen minutes of careful wiggling through the tangled undergrowth, they got to within sight of the camp. The hit wasn't going to be as easy as springing Phouma. Unlike the reeducation center, this camp was designed more like a prison. There was a string of razor wire, tight coils shoulder high, all around the perimeter. The buildings were more than thatched roofs on bamboo poles. They had walls, and there was no sign of any of the prisoners.

They couldn't even be sure Katherine May was here. Bolan was banking on Phouma's intelligence being accurate. If not, the chopper would have to go back without him. He could get a second pickup if he needed it, but he whispered a fervent hope that it wouldn't be necessary.

There was a gate of sorts, razor wire nailed to a movable wooden frame, and a solitary guard stood watch just inside. Taking him out would be no problem, but they couldn't afford to try it until they knew what they were up against. Bolan was aware of the finite amount of time at his disposal, but he had to be sure before they moved in. Most of all, he had to know where Katherine was.

The compound had been hacked out of the jungle and contained nine buildings, three on a side arranged in an open U shape. The wire ran fairly close to the buildings. Staying on the other side of it, they might be able to get near enough to see inside them, but only half were lighted, and those only barely.

Four of the buildings were watched by a pair of guards who meandered from one to another in a constant, shuffling patrol. Each had a light on inside. A fifth, the largest, sitting at the bottom of the U, was also lighted. It was probably the barracks. Bolan wondered if the dark buildings were unoccupied. If so, he might get lucky and get a glimpse of Katherine May.

He looked at his watch. One in the morning and counting. Ninety minutes to the chopper. He pulled Kwanh into the bushes and whispered what he wanted to do.

The Vietnamese nodded his understanding. "I'll work around the other side and check the building on the right," he whispered.

"All right. Be careful, and meet me back here in twenty minutes." Kwanh had to backtrack down the road in order to get across it without running the risk of being seen. But Bolan had three buildings to check. They were about even.

He explained the plan to Phouma. The Cambodian listened without comment. When Bolan was finished, Phouma confirmed that the largest building was indeed the barracks for the security unit. Then he said, "Leave the grenade launcher with me. If anything happens, I'll take out the barracks. Make sure you don't get near it."

Bolan handed him the rifle. The grenades were in Phouma's pack, and he knelt in the undergrowth to open the canvas bag. They only had four. Thin ice, but they had to skate on it. When Phouma was ready, the Executioner slipped into the undergrowth and worked his way toward the left-hand corner of the compound. In some places the edge of the jungle came to within ten or twelve feet of the razor wire, close enough to give him a good look into the huts.

As he inched past the corner, he was relieved to see a dim square of light on the outside wall of the first hut. That one, at least, had a window. He crept as near to the wire as he dared. As far as he could tell, it wasn't rigged with an alarm, but to get too far out in the open would risk blowing it all.

He couldn't see much of the interior of the room. There was no motion, no shadow, nothing to fix his eye on. The hut appeared deserted. He couldn't be sure, but he couldn't stay there all night, either. Instead, he moved on to the next hut, keeping one eye on the window. If he saw movement, he could try to get back.

The second hut was a little more active. Shadows danced on the wall—two of them—but they were vague, almost indistinguishable from each other. As near as he could tell, both occupants were men, but he couldn't be sure even of that. In profile only the breasts and the haircut would give him a clue. But the women incarcerated at the other camps were so wasted by starvation, whatever curves they had once had were long gone, melted away with their dignity and their freedom. And many of them had had their hair cut short to keep down the infestation of vermin.

He waited a little longer, hoping to get a glimpse of a face or two, but as the seconds ticked by, he felt time pressing against his back like a giant hand, pushing him on to the next hut.

It was his last.

He didn't expect to have any better luck this time and figured Kwanh would also come up empty. It wasn't the end of the world, but it came damn close. They'd have to take the time to search the huts one by one.

Here, too, there were shadows. One was moving; the other lay against the wall, bent in two and motionless, as unforgettable and lifeless a testimonial as those horrific shadows etched on the stone walls of Hiroshima, unspeakably eloquent even in their frozen immobility.

The moving shadow came close. For a moment he couldn't see hair, or a face, and there wasn't enough of the figure revealed to be certain of gender, let alone identity. Then the figure moved, and a cascade of long black hair tumbled into view.

It was Katherine May. It had to be. The hair was almost a dead giveaway. He'd seen several photos of Clayton Bishop's briefing and, aside from the perfect symmetry of her face, it was Katherine May's hair that struck a person. Model-shiny and perfectly brushed, it had looked like a sheet of black satin in the photos. Now her hair was full of tangles and snippets of vegetation, but there was no mistaking it. Then the woman near the edge of the window turned and all doubt was swept away.

He backed away, slipping into the undergrowth, the clock in his head ticking away. He looked at his watch.

One hour. All the time in the world, and not nearly enough to do what he had to do.

Phouma and Kwanh were motionless as the trees.

"You found her," Kwanh stated as Bolan joined the two men.

The warrior nodded. "It's show time."

Bolan was concerned. The two guards pacing the middle of the compound near the huts had vanished. Phouma said they were there one minute, strutting across the grounds, and the next thing he knew, they were gone. That was a problem, but he couldn't deal with it now.

The guard on the gate was his main focus. The road led right up to the gate, but it funneled outward about twenty-five yards before hitting the fence. Positioned behind the gate, the guard was well clear of cover on either side. A close approach was all but impossible. Hitting him at medium range wasn't an insurmountable problem, but Bolan wanted to know the next step before he took the first one.

The moonlight was still fairly bright, and he used binoculars to examine the gate itself. Flimsy, it would have posed no problem to a jeep, but they had had to go in on foot. A simple chain and padlock was used to keep it closed, but they had no bolt cutters. The meandering coils of razor wire made vaulting the barrier out of the question. Checking the lock as closely as he could, Bolan decided the Beretta might do the trick.

It would have to.

Creeping to the very edge of the undergrowth, he dropped into a shooting crouch and used a two-handed grip. The guard seemed restless and moved back and forth behind the gate. Bolan timed him and watched patiently as the guard moved to one end of his beat, then back, pivoting again like a mechanical bear in a shooting gallery.

Bolan held his breath, counting the paces, waiting for the one split second of immobility before the turn. The guard made his closest approach and froze. Bolan squeezed the trigger.

The Beretta spit twice and the guard staggered backward, his hands fluttering like butterfly wings just under his chin, then he folded up like a crepe paper Halloween skeleton and sat down in a heap. He teetered, started to fall and finally curled his head toward his lap and sat still.

Bolan, Kwanh and Phouma swarmed out of the jungle like angry locusts. Bolan fired twice, shattering the lock. Moving the gate wasn't going to be quite so easy. The wire was massed in front of the wooden frame. A bamboo pole jutted out on the inside, making a convenient handle. There was nothing to be done from outside the fence but grabbing the wire and lifting. They couldn't push, because the wire would just collapse toward the frame, rearranging its razor edges and folding around the hands of anyone who tried, like the jaws of a carnivorous plant trapping an unwary fly.

Phouma and Kwanh grabbed handfuls of the glittering coils, one at either end of the gate, and Bolan grabbed the middle. On a nod they lifted, pulling the gate outward and opening a gap wide enough for them to slip through. They left it only slightly ajar in case someone from the barracks happened to glance outside.

There was nothing they could do about the absence of the guard. Bolan grabbed the body under the shoulders and dragged it toward the first hut on the left, where he laid it on the ground in the shadows.

Phouma knelt at the corner of the building and trained the grenade launcher on the barracks. Bolan hoped it wouldn't have to be used. When Phouma was ready, the warrior led Kwanh on tiptoe along the back of the row of huts. The other guards were nowhere in sight, but they could appear at any moment. If Bolan could get Katherine out through the rear window, he might get her all the way out of the camp without firing another shot. Once she was in the clear, they could take the place apart at long range.

But it didn't work that way.

As the Executioner moved between the second and third huts, he heard a startled grunt. Turning, he saw one of the missing guards backing out from between the two buildings, tugging at his pants.

The second guard was on his knees, his pants down around his ankles. Hamstrung by the pants, he was struggling to get up and cover himself. The woman on the ground made no attempt to adjust her own clothing. In a flash Bolan realized what was going on. He raised the Beretta, but the moving guard ducked around the corner of the building before the warrior could pull the trigger.

Bolan switched targets and fired once, shooting the second guard through the forehead. The woman didn't even scream. She continued to lie there as if she were paralyzed. Bolan looked once to make sure it wasn't Katherine, and when he was sure it wasn't, he raced after the fleeing sentry.

As Bolan leaped over the prostrate form of the woman, a shout echoed across the open space and bounced around between the buildings. Thinking quickly, the guard then fired a short burst to attract attention.

Bright lights flooded the compound in a matter of seconds. As Bolan peered around the corner, he saw the guard running for the barracks. There was no point in being quiet now, and the warrior swung around his M-16. He fired a burst, hosing the muzzle in the general direction of the running sentry. Pushed along by the impact of the slugs, the man seemed to leap forward a few feet, then pitched headlong as his torso outran his legs. He sprawled on his face and slid a few feet across the damp ground.

Soldiers were already spilling out of the barracks. They spread out as Bolan opened up with the M-16. A sustained burst took two down, but the rest hit the deck and scampered for cover.

There was a sudden resonant krumping sound, as if someone had struck a huge empty barrel, and the front of the barracks blew out as Phouma's first grenade found its mark. Kwanh slid down behind the third hut as Bolan leaped to his feet and charged down the front. The M-16 blazing on his hip, he slammed his back against the raw timber of the front door. It didn't give at first, and he stepped forward to try again. This time he heard something creak as the door started to rip its frame loose. On the third try the door crashed inward and fell flat, Bolan on top of it as the first sporadic bursts of return fire slashed at the front of the hut.

The thatch walls offered little resistance, and several slugs ripped through, passed over his head and out the back of the hut.

Bolan rolled onto his belly and scrambled away from the door. He heard Kwanh's AK start to chatter from the front corner as he scanned the room. In the corner, her hands covering her ears, sat Katherine May.

He called her name, but she didn't respond immediately. He started toward her when there was a second explosion over near the barracks. The brilliant lights of the compound flickered, went very dim, flared brightly again, then went out altogether.

Bolan scrambled on all fours toward the corner. He found Katherine in the dark, grabbed her arm as he stood and hauled her to her feet. She struggled to pull free, and Bolan had to drag her to the door, all the while trying to reassure her that he was there to free her. She clawed at the back of his hand, trying desperately to break his hold, but he was too strong for her.

Finally she surrendered, and he wrapped his arms around her, whispering that everything was all right, that she was safe.

"But you have to do exactly as I say," he warned her. He felt her head against his shoulder, nodding that she understood. A third explosion shattered the momentary calm, then Kwanh's AK started hammering again.

Bolan pulled the woman with him, reached the doorway and looked out into the camp. Several bodies were strewn across the front of the ruined barracks. In three or four places little comets of light spit at Kwanh's position. He couldn't see the Khmer Rouge, but he knew they were there.

Phouma had one more grenade left, and after that it would be bullet to bullet and, if it came to it, hand to hand. Bolan glanced at his watch. The illuminated dial showed it was one-forty. Twenty minutes to pick up. He had to get Katherine away now before she got hit with a stray bullet.

"Kwanh!" he shouted.

The Vietnamese didn't answer. He called again, but this time an explosion of concentrated fire from across the compound drowned out everything but its own thunder. The Khmer Rouge were using tracers, and Bolan followed the spears of red and green back to the points of origin. He dropped to one knee just inside the hut and waited for the next burst, which came almost immediately. He snaked a double arc of fire across the open ground, circling one firing position. The tracers stopped.

More fire, this time slicing at the hut. He dropped to the floor, pulling Katherine down with him. Once more he took his time and emptied the rest of his clip at another hidden Khmer Rouge. A second line of tracers winked out and didn't reappear.

There was no way to tell how many men were hidden on the other side, but it was dead certain they wouldn't stay put for long. If they had a competent commander, he'd already be planning an assault across the compound, probably slipping behind the flaming barracks and trying to come up on Bolan and Kwanh from behind.

He called to the Vietnamese a third time and was answered.

"We're coming out," Bolan told him, "through the back wall. Meet us there."

Without waiting for an answer he turned away from the doorway, rammed a new clip into the M-16 and sliced a burst vertically, slitting the thatching as if he were using a laser. Jumping to his feet, he hauled Katherine up bodily and dragged her toward the back wall. He picked up speed, then slammed into the leafy wall and plunged through to the other side. He lost his balance and fell heavily. Katherine, dragged through the opening behind him, tripped over his outstretched body and planted both knees in the small of his back. The collision knocked the breath from his lungs, and he gasped for air as Kwanh rounded the corner.

The little man bent to help Katherine to her feet, and Bolan, still fighting the searing vacuum in his chest, got to his knees. Kwanh took the woman by the hand and started pulling her. Bolan planted a hand in the middle of her back and pushed her forward. As he made it to his feet and started to run, the first two Khmer Rouge rounded the corner of the hut and opened fire.

Bolan spun around as the hail of AK slugs scratched and clawed at the gaping wall of ruptured thatch partially obscuring the two raiders and their prize.

Bolan held the M-16 in one hand and waved it back and forth. The magazine emptied and the receiver locked open. Backing up at full speed, he tossed the empty away, as casually as a drunken sailor disposing of an empty beer bottle, and inserted a fresh clip.

The attackers stopped in their tracks at the edge of the sundered wall, and Bolan dropped them both with a short, brutal burst fired waist high, pumping enough heavy metal to cut the men to shreds.

Then he turned and sprinted across the compound.

IN THE NEAR DISTANCE Bolan could see Katherine May trailing along behind Kwanh, wobbling in her flight like the tail of a runaway kite. Another Khmer

Rouge soldier rounded the corner, and the warrior stopped just long enough to loose a burst, driving the soldier back behind the last hut.

The toughest part was still to come. Kwanh and Katherine disappeared around the side of a hut, and Bolan raced after them. It was a good twenty to twenty-five yards to the gate, flat, open and deadly. Phouma realized their predicament and charged toward the gate. He had an AK in one hand and the grenade launcher in the other.

Bolan heard footsteps charging along the back of the huts and ducked around the corner, the M-16 blazing on full-auto. In the darkness he couldn't see anyone, but the footsteps stopped and he shouted, "Kwanh! Go, go, go!"

The Vietnamese headed into the open as Phouma laid down selective covering fire, not trying so much to hit anyone as to make sure the Khmer Rouge stayed put. Katherine was petrified and didn't follow until Bolan gave her a shove. But once she started moving, the terror took over and she passed Kwanh on the way to the gate. Bolan swept the open compound with the muzzle of the M-16, but the field was empty.

Katherine was through the gate now, and Bolan saw Phouma wave her past, shouting something in Cambodian. Kwanh was next, and he slipped through, positioning himself a few yards past the narrow opening.

Now it was Bolan's turn.

Footsteps pounded behind him again, but this time he ignored them. The gunfire stopped for a moment and, hoping the sniping Khmer Rouge had to reload, Bolan made a break for it. He was halfway to the gate when a shout snapped at him from behind, and he almost missed a stride. The warrior saw Phouma get to his feet and dive through the open gate. His clothes snagged on the wire, but not enough to slow him down. The old man rolled once, then again, and lay supine.

He was wide to the left, and Bolan veered in toward the wire as Phouma started firing past him. Bolan dived through the opening and immediately turned to lay down covering fire for Phouma, who climbed to his feet and started backing toward the gate. Four Khmer Rouge charged toward him.

Phouma was just five feet from the gate when a slug caught him in the leg, just above the knee. He went down hard, letting go of his rifle as he fell. One of the Khmer Rouge soldiers shouted in exultation and sprinted past his comrades, firing back and forth until the magazine was empty.

Bolan closed his eyes for a second as Phouma's body bounced under the impact of bullet after bullet. He fanned his own rifle back and forth, nailing the charging soldier and taking out two of the three behind him. The last turned tail as Bolan's clip went dry. The big man headed toward the gate, but Kwanh grabbed him by the arm. "You can't help him."

Bolan knew that Phouma was dead, and knew, too, that the death was some sort of atonement, a sacrifice to make up in some small measure for the horror the old Cambodian had contributed to for so long. It wasn't enough, but it was a start.

"Come on," Kwanh begged. "We have to get back into the trees before they regroup."

Bolan nodded, bending to retrieve the grenade launcher, and loped toward the trees. Kwanh backed up all the way, firing two short bursts but without drawing any return fire.

As the Executioner reached the edge of the forest, a voice called, "Over here."

Katherine May stepped out of the trees, holding the spare Kalashnikov. She seemed to have recovered from her terror, or to have been pushed beyond it by the fury of the assault.

Bolan walked into the jungle, followed by Kwanh. The Executioner looked at his watch. Two minutes to go.

Before he could even say the words aloud, he heard the chopper. The familiar throbbing pulse was rising and falling on the wind as the aircraft approached.

Katherine looked confused. "What's happening?"

"There's a chopper coming to pick us up. We're getting the hell out of here. You'll be back in Thailand in two hours."

Suddenly something seemed to click in her head, and she looked at the Vietnamese more closely. "Colonel Kwanh . . . is that you?"

The sound of the chopper was growing progressively louder. The aircraft couldn't be more than a mile or two away. Bolan looked at Kwanh, waiting for his answer. Why was the Vietnamese hesitating?

Katherine asked again, as if it couldn't be true.

"Yes." It was almost a whisper. "Yes, it's me."

"But I thought...I don't understand. What's going on?" She turned to Bolan. "Who are you? Why are you here? With him?" She pointed to Kwanh with the AK. For a second Bolan thought she meant to use it.

The chopper arrived overhead suddenly, bright lights slashing down at the ground. Bolan waved and sprinted into the open. The chopper, a Huey without markings, started to descend, maneuvering over toward the wire to make sure the rotor tips cleared the trees.

Sporadic gunfire erupted from the interior of the camp. Several slugs glanced off the chopper, and Bolan heard the brutal hammering of an M-134 minigun as the door gunner let loose at the camp.

"Come on," Bolan shouted.

Kwanh was staring at Katherine. "You thought what?" He was yelling, and Bolan didn't know whether it was to make himself heard over the roar of the chopper's engines and the minigun or to somehow force the woman to answer the question. Maybe both.

"Tell me!" Kwanh shouted.

Bolan moved back toward them. He grabbed Katherine by the arm, but she pulled free.

"I thought you were the reason I was captured. I thought you were responsible for this." She waved a hand vaguely, taking in the razor wire, the litter of dead bodies and the burning wreckage of the camp. "I thought you had turned."

"But why?" Kwanh demanded. "How could you think that?"

"Trang," she replied.

"What about Trang?" Bolan, too, was immobilized now, listening intently.

"When I saw him, I thought that—"

"You *saw* him?"

She shook her head, more bewildered than ever. "Yes, I saw him here."

"Here?"

"He's in charge of this camp. He brought me here. He's—"

The chopper was exposed, and Bolan was getting impatient. They had a narrow margin as it was, and he couldn't wait any longer. He picked Katherine May up bodily and carried her to the aircraft. Two men in civilian attire leaned out of the chopper, and Bolan was surprised that one of them was Clayton Bishop. Bishop gave him a thumbs-up.

Bolan turned back to the Vietnamese. "Kwanh! Let's go!"

The Vietnamese shook his head. "I'm not going."

"You can't stay here."

"Go," Kwanh said. "I have to find Trang. He's the traitor. He's the one who set you up. He's responsible for all this, for Salang, all of it."

The Executioner took a step forward, but Kwanh backed away. He raised the muzzle of the AK, vaguely threatening as the assault rifle wavered in the air with a gentle motion, like an underwater plant in a swift current.

"Leave me," Kwanh said. "I'll be all right."

Bolan nodded curtly, then turned to climb into the chopper. Bishop gave him a hand, shouting to the pilot over his shoulder as he hauled the big man in.

Almost immediately the Huey started to lift off. The whole camp was ablaze now, the entire scene stained bright orange by the flames. He could see it all—nearly a dozen Khmer Rouge crouched in a tight knot near the end of the flaming barracks, now little more than a wall of flame and ruined timber; the obscene sprawl of a dozen dead men, their limbs so awkward in death they looked as if they were still in the act of dying; Phouma, the bloodstains from two dozen bullet holes merged in a single scarlet smear; and Kwanh, picking his way carefully through the narrow opening in the razor wire, a small figure made even smaller by the distance, shrinking as the chopper climbed.

A moment later the Huey wheeled away, and Kwanh slipped out of sight.

GOLD EAGLE

The Eagle now lands at different times at your retail outlet!

Be sure to look for your favorite action adventure from Gold Eagle on these dates each month.

Publication Month	In-Store Dates
May	April 24
June	May 22
July	June 19
August	July 24

We hope that this new schedule will be convenient for you.

Please note: There may be slight variations in on-sale dates in your area due to differences in shipping and handling. GEDATES-R

TAKE 'EM NOW

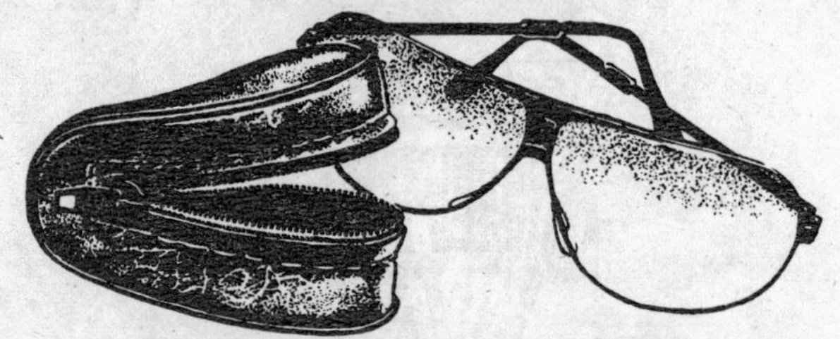

FOLDING SUNGLASSES FROM GOLD EAGLE

Mean up your act with these tough, street-smart shades. Practical, too, because they fold 3 times into a handy, zip-up polyurethane pouch that fits neatly into your pocket. Rugged metal frame. Scratch-resistant acrylic lenses. Best of all, they can be yours for only $6.99.

MAIL YOUR ORDER TODAY.

Send your name, address, and zip code, along with a check or money order for just $6.99 + .75¢ for delivery (for a total of $7.74) payable to Gold Eagle Reader Service. (New York residents please add applicable sales tax.)

Remove from pouch..

unfold once.

unfold twice.

and they're ready to wear.

Gold Eagle Reader Service
3010 Walden Avenue
P.O. Box 1396
Buffalo, N.Y. 14240-1396

GES-1AR

Offer not available in Canada.

OKLAHOMA'S FINEST—THE MEANEST, TOUGHEST BUNCH OF ROUGH RIDERS—HIT THE SOUTH OF FRANCE. . . .

OKLAHOMA

COMPANY OF HEROES

William Reed

The action-packed, authentic account of America's National Guard continues in BOOK 2 of SOLDIERS OF WAR.

This time, the focus is on Dog Company—the fiercest unit of the Thunderbirds of Oklahoma. They are bound by blood and driven by the fighting spirit that tamed a wild land—and facing tough odds to save the Allied effort in this exciting World War II action.

Available in July at your favorite retail outlet, or order your copy by sending your name, address, zip or postal code along with a check or money order for $3.50, plus 75¢ postage and handling ($1.00 in Canada), payable to Gold Eagle Books to:

In the U.S.	**In Canada**
Gold Eagle Books	Gold Eagle Books
3010 Walden Ave.	P.O. Box 609
P.O. Box 1325	Fort Erie, Ontario
Buffalo, NY 14269-1325	L2A 5X3

Please specify book title with your order.
Canadian residents add applicable federal and provincial taxes.

SOW2-1RR